Web of the Trio

Thanks for Coming
Lilian Amushan
06/05/16.

Nnenna Lilian Amushan

Copyright © Nnenna Lilian Amushan 2016

First Published in Ireland, in 2016, in co-operation with Choice Publishing, Drogheda, County Louth, Republic of Ireland.
www.choicepublishing.ie

ISBN: 978-1-911131-06-9 (Paperback)
ISBN: 978-1-911131-95-3 (Ebook)

All rights reserved. No part of this publication may be reproduced, stored in a retrieval system, or transmitted, in any form or by any means, electronic, mechanical, photocopying, recording or otherwise, without the prior permission of the copyright holder.

This novel is entirely a work of fiction.
The names, characters and incidents portrayed in it are the work of the author's imagination. Any resemblance to actual persons, living or dead, events or localities is entirely coincidental.

A catalogue record for this book is available from the National Library

I dedicate this novel to:

All people in Diaspora.

A lot of people leave their countries not because they really want to, but because of the circumstances they find themselves in.

Some seek security, better life and peace of mind or even adventure.

1

Lagos 1972

The bus eventually arrived Lagos in the evening and the passengers gratefully got down, stretched before carrying their different loads and headed for their various destinations.

Among these passengers was Joe Mbakwe, a young man in his mid twenties, one of the thousands of people who had just graduated from the university and had come to Lagos to find a well-paid job and maybe, quick money. He believed he would make it, he had been poor all his life and he wanted a change. He had struggled, got through the university with a B.A. in Marketing.

He carried his luggage and stared around him, smiling optimistically as he made his way to board a bus that would take him to Ajegunle, where he would stay temporarily with a friend. He eventually found the place after some enquiries. He knocked on the wooden door of the small house that looked just like the others. It was an area for the less privileged ones, Joe thought wryly as he knocked again. The door creaked open and Mike grinned widely at him.

'Hey buddy!' he said slapping Joe on the back,

'Welcome to my little hole! You eventually made the journey.'

'Mike, it's so nice to see you! I thought I would never reach my destination, this is the longest journey I've ever made,' Joe said as he came inside the one-bedroom apartment and dropped his luggage on the floor.

'Make yourself at home Joe, remember that this is your home until you find a job. Joe, this is Lagos, you really have to run around and find yourself a job. Every year thousands of graduates like you troop into Lagos hunting for jobs. Anyway,' he shrugged, 'you've always been a lucky guy. You'll soon land yourself somewhere good and when you do so, don't forget me o!'

Joe smiled; 'Do you think I can make it?'

'Of course you can, if you run around and contact the right people.'

* * * * * * *

Sonny Adele came out of the Black Honda. He

was carrying his briefcase. It was Monday morning; work was always hectic on Mondays. He entered the magnificent building with the sign 'KK and Co.' It was an import and export company. The offices were already alive and bustling with people. He entered his office, his secretary, a woman in her early thirties had already put the place in order, but she wasn't there at the moment. Sonny checked the files. At ten o'clock, there would be a meeting of the board of directors, the Masters of the Underworld. It was still 7.30 a.m. and he had to crosscheck some things before the meeting.

It was 9.55 a.m. but in the conference room on the top most floor of KK and Co, more than twenty men sat round the conference table. Only one seat was vacant and they were waiting for the person that was supposed to occupy it. Without him, the meeting would not hold, unless he sent a representative, which he had never done. However, KK Johnson arrived at 10.00 a.m. on the dot and with capable strides went over to his seat. Just as he came in, the atmosphere in the room changed. They all stood up and chanted their anthem in low but deep voices. It had a strong tune and it always reflected on their faces as they sang:

*'We are the Masters: we are one
Masters of yesterday, today and tomorrow
Invincible we vow, today and always....'*

'I want the important reports.' KK Johnson said after they had chanted the anthem and sat down. Okoh stood up. He was a small man in his early thirties. He had a baldhead and his skull was roughly sculptured and looked rather thick.

'The operation went well sir; our boys really got Chief Alaka wetting his pants with fear. With the pictures he is ours and if Chief Alaka plus the few others are ours, the state government is ours.' He sat down as KK and a few others silently nodded in agreement.

'I would like to have a copy of the picture,' KK Johnson said to Okoh. He nodded. Another man, Alan stood up.

'I heard a rumour from one of our girls that the Vikings are planning to adopt another method to destroy us totally. She said that from what they were discussing, it is a slow poison that would take up to twenty years to wipe us completely out.'

'This is no report!' KK said in his slow drawl. 'You have to find out more. Be specific on the method. The girls are not doing their job. Meanwhile, one person only should be given a job in this company this year. Only one person, a fresh, intelligent person who will appreciate it... he is going to be a Master. Any objections to what I've just said?' he slowly looked around and continued. Nobody opposed him.

'I think that would be the best thing, until we straightened out our clash with Vikings. We all know that we have only thirty-four families as members of this organization whereas the Vikings have more than eighty, and other organizations, have not less than forty to fifty families, but then brethren, we all should also look at the quality point of view and not always at quantity....'

*   *   *   *   *   *   *

Joe Mbakwe finished writing the third letter of application. He put it in the third envelope and sealed it. It was Monday morning, his third day in Lagos. The morning paper, from which he had seen the vacancies, was still beside him. After he had addressed the envelopes, he sealed them, and taking them with him, he locked the door and went down the street in search of a post office. He had better ask for direction, if he wants to land himself in a post office. He went inside the little shop in front of the third house. A beautiful girl was at the counter. The girl was really beautiful despite her simple dressing. She should be around twenty-two or twenty-three years old. There was no other person in the shop.

'Yes, can I help you?' asked the girl behind the counter.

'Em... I'm new here and I don't really know my way around. Where can I find the nearest post office?' Joe asked, inclining a bit on the counter.

'There is one at Adeyuba Street. Just go straight ahead, then take the second turn by your left, then you can still ask around when you get there.'

'Thanks. I am Joe.'

'I'm Marina.' *Marina. Marina.* Joe kept thinking about her all through the day. There was something special about her which he couldn't pin point.

Some minutes past 7.00 p.m., Mike came back from work, he worked in a fuel station.

'So how was your day?' Joe asked him.

'Hectic as usual, there was a big rush because of this fuel scarcity. They all kept stuffing me with tips and I didn't know to whom I would sell first. How about you, have you made any moves?'

'Wrote three letters of application and posted.'

'Ha! Letters of application! My friend, if you're serious, you had better get on your feet and go from office to office in search of a job otherwise the long-legged ones would get it first. You have your certificate, a good one at that and you also have your good looks.' Mike said as he sat down on the tattered but clean couch and removed his shirt, which he threw across the room to a chair.

'Which companies did you apply to?'

'Okon trading company, em... I can't really remember their names; all these Yoruba names keep confusing me.'

'I know one company that takes the maximum of three people a year. Their pay is very high but anyway, I don't think they would consider you, you don't have connections,' he shrugged casually 'moreover, I don't think they have vacancies. Have you eaten dinner?' he asked with a loud yawn. But Joe's mind was already racing 'What's the name of the company?'

The next day Joe Mbakwe went into a shop and bought some used pairs of trousers, shirts, a tie and jacket. He ironed them until they were crisp, polished his fairly worn black shoe until they shone. He was ready to visit the company the next day, Wednesday.

In the evening he strolled down the road to the little shop. Marina was there and she smiled at him when he entered.

'I hope you didn't find it difficult to locate the post office yesterday?' she asked.

'No, it wasn't difficult to locate. Do you mind if I

kept you company?'

The clock at the outer office where Joe was told to wait, chimed eight o'clock. He had arrived 'KK and Co', at exactly a quarter to eight. The offices were slowly filling up. Everybody passed him, oblivious of him. He prayed they would give him a job in this beautiful building. He was the only person in the room, which had a desk, a chair and two settees. It also had a fan and two windows. The entire floor was beautifully tiled, neat and well polished. Twenty minutes later, the secretary came out from the inner office.

'Oh I'm sorry, I was so busy I forgot I kept you waiting,' she said dumping some papers on the desk.

'What can we do for you?'

'I want a job. I mean if there's vacancy.'

'Where are your credentials?'

Joe brought out his papers and handed them to her. She sceptically glanced through them.

'Hundreds of people have done what you just did; they've come here looking for jobs. Your cert. is OK but I don't think we have any vacancy. Wait a minute.' She went inside the inner office again. After a short while she came out with a paper and shook her head. 'You might just be lucky. There is vacancy, which was released on Monday but has not yet been placed on newspapers if they're going to place it. But you have to wait for Mr. Sonny Adele, my boss.'

Joe heaved a sigh of relief. 'Thank you,' he said with a smile, 'I'm ready to wait the whole day.'

Joe waited for two hours and Sonny eventually came to the office. When he entered the office, Joe's instinct told him 'Yes, this is the Sonny' and he was right. Joe could smell wealth and that was exactly what Sonny smelt of. His shoes were superb and his suit was something else. He barely glanced at Joe as he strode inside his office. A few minutes later, Joe was called into the office. He was alone with Sonny.

'Have a seat,' Sonny said in a businesslike voice. 'I'm Sonny Adele.'

'Joe Mbakwe.' The two men shook hands.

'Joe, you might be lucky. I've seen your papers.' Joe nodded. Sonny looked hard at him for some seconds, assessing, weighing.

'Well, you have to elaborate on your c.v. Our company is a bit different, we are very careful about whom we employ. We would like to know every single detail of your past, don't exclude anything. If you can bring it tomorrow, then you come back next week, by this time. You might be interviewed.'

'Yes sir.'

'10.00 a.m. next week, be punctual.'

Joe left the office. His level of optimism was a bit lowered with all these '*mights.*' '*You might be lucky, you might be interviewed*'

Sonny dialled the phone in his office. He was calling the boys assigned to him.

'I need you to keep watch on a guy called Joe Mbakwe. Come to my office straight away to collect his address and some basic information. Find out everything,' he spoke into the receiver. After that, he called KK Johnson and reported about the job hunter.

The next day, Joe wrote the summary of his life, it wasn't much, nothing much has happened in his life. He didn't go into much detail lest he gave the impression that he was not suitable for the job. He had lived most part of his life struggling to make ends meet. He was brought up in Umudike village in the Eastern region of Nigeria. When he finished secondary school his parents died mysteriously and he was alone with no brothers or sisters, only selfish uncles who wanted to get hold of his father's little properties which he left behind. Joe had to sell most of the properties, and with the meagre amount, he got through the university. He also did some part time menial jobs during the holidays, and now he has graduated and wanted a job.

Joe's next meeting with Sonny was the next six days. It seemed such a long time to Joe who kept praying that somebody else would not take the job. He spent the next six days with Marina at their little shop. Sometimes Marina would come to his temporary home and they'd spend some time together. They had learnt quite a lot about each other just within a week. Marina had finished her secondary school and harbours this dream of owning a boutique, of being a very big businesswoman. She had confided in Joe.

2

It was Wednesday morning. By eight o'clock, Joe was on his way to Victoria Island, premises of KK and Co. At exactly ten o'clock he was called inside Sonny's office.

'I like punctuality. Have a seat,' Sonny said as Joe entered the office. Sonny began without preamble. His voice was businesslike. Joe thought Sonny looked different today, he looked hard and mean although his face was relaxed.

'You are not married.' It was a statement rather than a question. 'If you are going to be fully employed, you have to be a married man.' Sonny shifted closer on his chair 'whatever questions I ask you, I would expect a straightforward answer. But first of all let me warn you Mr. Mbakwe,' his face was stern, his gaze cold and intent. 'If you are not interested in what I have to tell you, you quickly find your way back and forget you ever saw my face and pretend that this meeting never existed. This is for your own good.' He paused to let his words sink in.

'Now let's get down to business. My first question is to what extent would you go in order to get money, to have money in abundance? Are you ready to do anything for money... hard, cold, cash?'

'Is this part of the interview?' Joe asked in disbelief.

'Mr. Mbakwe, you haven't answered my question.'

'No... I mean yes. I'll do almost anything…, it depends....'

'Almost? Ha! Don't try to be smart, boy! I told you I want a direct answer.' Sonny's gaze was boring into Joe's eyes. Joe could see something dangerous; he looked like a complete psychopath.

'Yes. I'll do anything for money.' Joe's voice shook slightly as he spoke. *God! Am I crazy?*

'Follow me'

They used the elevator and got to the topmost floor of the seven-storey building. 'We are going to the conference room,' Sonny said. About nine people were sitting round the table, talking among themselves. Sonny entered first and Joe followed him. Every conversation came to a halt as they entered and all eyes were on Joe. They were assessing him. He felt completely ill at ease.

'This is the man,' Sonny said, gesturing towards Joe. 'He is Joe as you all know,' then to

Joe he said 'these people you see here are some of the members of board of directors of this company. We all are called the Masters of the Underworld. We own this company.'

'You said Masters of the Underworld?' Joe asked, he thought they were just joking but their faces were serious.

'Joe sit down, we are going to have a long meeting.'

Joe wondered again, but didn't speak. It was only when the meeting started that he fully realized he had just joined a notorious organization, there was no going back although he hadn't been formally recognized as one of the members. It was really a long meeting; the discussions were strange to Joe who understood nothing. After some time, a man who introduced himself as Okoh, asked him some series of questions which he answered.

'You are expected to come here every morning, except on Sundays. Each week, a certain task is assigned and you dare not leave the task undone. Don't tremble, nobody will ask you to kill,' this last statement made the others to laugh. Okoh continued.

'You will spend three years' probation period, during which you will receive only half of your salary. It is quite a generous amount of money. You are expected to marry within two months.

Your family just like ours must not mix with people. We only mix with each other. We, the Masters of the Underworld are scattered all over Nigeria and abroad, here in Lagos we have more than thirty families as members.'

Joe wished he could withdraw but knew it was impossible.

'Look! I don't know why you're fidgeting, but there is no going back mister!' his laughter and a few others echoed in the silent room, 'unless you want to have a small *accident* on your way back.' His expression was deadly again as he continued.

'Listen and listen very carefully, I haven't finished. After we must have chanted our anthem, you'll take a vow which would be recorded, promising this society that you will abide by all its rules and regulations and that you will NEVER EVER betray this organization. This vow is no child's play. Once you have taken this vow, you belong to this society. Break the vow and face the consequences, betray us and you will not live to tell the tale.' He continued in his powerful baritone voice.

'You have a lot to learn about this organization and you will know everything within this probation period. After the probation, you'll then be in control like us, and you will start earning full salary. You will also vow that when the probation is over, your next child, whether male or female, must marry a member of this society at the age of twenty. At the age of twenty-one, the child takes over and you'll formally retire at the age of fifty, after you have guided your child. Nobody plays games with the Masters and gets away with it. If your wife delivers no child two years after probation, you'll be used as a sacrifice. We are not going to kill you, but then we will make your life so miserable you'll contemplate suicide.'

Joe was in a daze. It was too much for him. He screamed 'No!' but the man just smiled. Joe looked around at their faces and wondered how they all got to join this organization. He looked at Sonny who nodded and flashed him a complacent smile. Okoh continued.

'About the child that would take over, whether male or female, make sure he does not mix with other people. If he has to go to school, secondary school level should be the maximum...'

Joe could barely hear the last words.

'... now time to take the vow.'

A month later....

'But its too early Joe,' Marina tried to convince him. Joe had proposed to her. They were in Joe's new apartment in Victoria Island. The company gave it to him during his first week at work.

'It is not. Marina, I need you in my life. I know I just got a job, a house and a car the other day but....'

'It's not that. I mean I want you to get used to being rich before I marry you. I don't want to compete with anything or anybody,' Marina said, standing up. She paced slowly across the room.

'Marina I want us to marry really soon. I don't want to lose you. Why won't you understand or don't you love me? If you don't, just say it Marina, just say it.' He stood up and faced Marina, boring his eyes into hers 'say it, Marina. Don't you love me or are you afraid? Yes, she's afraid. I can see fear in your eyes Marina, fear that you might make a mistake marrying me....'

'Joe, I'll marry you. I love you,' Marina burst out. Joe held her closer. Everything was complete. He heaved a sigh of relief.

'I love you Marina. Thanks,' he whispered 'thanks.'

Joe was gradually getting used to being a Master. He had worked for two years. One more year and his probation period would end. Since the past couple of years, Joe had undergone some series of metamorphosis. It was initially hard for him, but as time passed he started making the best of the bad situation, since there was no way out. He had learnt a lot of things about the organization. It was a very powerful organization and a large one, which existed in Nigeria, and some other African countries since the early 1920's. As the society expanded, it became more powerful and notorious. All through the years it existed, no one really believed they existed except those they had really dealt directly with, men at the top. Others took it as one of those fabricated stories about secret societies.

In Lagos, there was a time they had been blackmailing one of the most influential businessmen for three years. Blackmail was what they specialized in. They would set you up and you would be theirs. They would then use you to get whatever they wanted. They had the government in their palms. Anyway, the businessman was almost reduced to complete poverty when he decided to investigate the organization. He did everything in his power to dissolve the society but before he was murdered, he found out that the society was truly invincible.

It was anarchic in a revolutionary kind of way. They believed that individual freedom should be absolute and all government and law are evil. They were quite dogmatic in their beliefs. The Masters were more or less like 'Blackhand', an extortion racket which operated in the USA in the late eighteenth century. That was all before the war, during the civil war, the society collapsed mysteriously, but just after the war, the notorious KK Johnson revived it. The Masters now want to be as powerful as they previously were.

Joe was assigned a new task each week. Most of the tasks were very risky ones but he left none undone. He proved to be a very active member and the powers of the society were intriguing him, the way they blackmailed and manipulated top officials in the government. They rarely demanded money from them, what they demanded mostly were favours.

At the moment, their target is Justice Remo, the Judge in charge of John's case. John is a son of one of the Masters. He was caught with hard drugs and the final hearing would be in two weeks' time. They knew what the verdict would be and they were determined to set John free. They only had to get Remo and John would be set free.

The case was assigned to Joe, and Sonny was to supervise. They were in Sonny's office and had already laid out their plans. Earlier, the boys assigned to Sonny had brought the information that Justice Remo had a mistress who was his former house girl. They had a secret hideout in the outskirts of Lagos, but the thing that thrilled Joe most was that they had photographs and video that would bring disaster to Remo's life.

*   *   *   *   *   *   *   *

She sat tersely on the settee in the sitting room. Everywhere was silent except the tick of the clock on the wall. She was lonesome. Twelve-month-old Chidi was peacefully asleep upstairs. Her beautiful face devoid of make-up, thoughtful eyes and pursed lips, depicted a picture more or less like Mona Lisa.

Marina Mbakwe was miles away. Her thought centred on her husband, Joe, her marriage, strange behaviours, something was very wrong but she couldn't guess. Her mind drifted back to her wedding day. It was a small affair but well organized. Joe had been very excited. Their honeymoon would always remain green in her memory, two weeks of pure bliss. It was a pity that Joe had to resume work after the wedding. During his first two or three months at work, there wasn't much problems. He would return home for lunch most afternoons, and he would always come back from the office before seven-thirty p.m. He would always call from his office to ask her how she was doing and they would talk for a while. She didn't feel very lonely then. But there were many things she didn't understand about him, about his job.

He never discussed his job, made strict rules about her friends. He said that for reasons best known to them, all families under KK and Co interact only with themselves. Marina had made friends with many of them. She was close to Mrs. Kate Adele, Sonny's wife. She had confided in her. In the swimming pool one hot Tuesday afternoon, Marina had mentioned her problems to Kate.

'You know Marina,' Kate had said, 'we all had the same problem during the first years of our marriages. We are like one family, the KK and Co, we all have rules binding us together, the company is different, and it is not like others. It is a bit more dignified and very soon, Marina you'll get used to us. When you have a baby, you will just forget about all these things.'

'I just hope things would get better, Kate. This is not the life I dreamt of when I got married to Joe. I'm even thinking of opening a boutique....'

'That is a nice idea but you have to find somebody to run the place.' Kate cut in as she went towards the pool.

'I would run it myself of course, that would keep me busy, and thanks for your suggestion, Kate,' Marina said curtly.

'It is not a suggestion, it is a rule, a law, an order.' She went inside the pool and started swimming.

Marina's problems and worries got worse when she gave birth to Chidi. She was worried that Joe wasn't excited, as a new daddy should be. What worried her most was that Joe rarely came home for lunch and he kept late nights. But she didn't think Joe was unfaithful to her, or did she think so?

She got up and paced slowly in the room. She had gone through Joe's belongings, looked for signs or anything that was suspicious or perfume that might be lingering on his shirt, but nothing. So what could it be? The clock chimed softly, echoing through the whole house. Marina looked at it, 11.00 p.m. She went upstairs and checked tiny Chidi who was still sleeping peacefully. She then went to their bedroom. It was imperative that she talked with Joe, but she knew Joe would be tired when he comes back. She would wait.

Lagos 1975

All of a sudden Joe changed to a family man. He was once again the man Marina married. Marina leaned on the doorpost as she watched her husband play with his son, Chidi on the front lawn. They were playing football. Marina felt so happy; moreover, their eight-month-old baby was kicking happily in her womb. A self-satisfactory smile played on her lips. She was happy.

'Chidi you never get tired,' Joe said as he slapped his son gently on the back. Chidi was an exact replica of Marina. 'Now you go and take your bath.'

'But daddy...' Joe shook his head.

'Daddy will play with you tomorrow,' Marina told Chidi who picked up his ball and raced upstairs with his sturdy legs.

'And how is our baby?' Joe asked Marina as they went inside.

'Kicking happily.'

Joe smiled. His probation period ended last month and the baby Marina was carrying would replace him. The baby would be a Master when it is twenty-one and it didn't excite Joe, but it was inevitable.

Two weeks later Marina had a baby girl. They called her Pearl. Joe carried the tiny bundle in his arms and stared at the child who would later take over his business. She would be a Master. Joe wished it were male. He heard the front door open and turned to face Sonny who was grinning at him. He was carrying a package.

'Congrats Joe! I just came back from Port Harcourt this morning and Kate told me. Came at the right time huh?'

'You mean the baby? Yes. Just at the right

time, but I wish it were a boy.'

Oh' Sonny smiled, 'you're very lucky. Girls are vulnerable all you have to do is to be very close to her and train her up to do whatever you say, but the only thing is to make her ignorant of the business until she is about nineteen years.'

Joe sighed. 'This is difficult.'

'Yes. But you know the alternative.'

Joe called the nanny, and handed the baby to her.

'Meanwhile here is a present for the little girl,' Sonny said, dropping the package on a table. Without waiting for an answer he continued, but his voice changed to a businesslike tone, 'the men we sent yesterday messed up the whole deal....'

'Let's go to my study, you know that is where I talk business.'

3

'Is it so serious?' Joe was pacing about and now he turned to face Sonny.

'It is no big deal. The devil is not as black as you paint it. I can tell you that behind that mean facade lies a soft man.'

'That is what you think, better get ready for anything. Do you realize how much money we lost? I think you're taking it too lightly but this is a very serious thing,' Joe said.

'And hardly our fault for goodness' sake! Nobody should blame us just because the boys messed up the deal. They were too careless.'

The prospect of being queried by the notorious KK Johnson sent a wave of goose pimples down Joe's spine. They sat tersely on the back seat as the driver pulled the black sleek Mercedes to a halt in front of the huge gates. A security man in uniform emerged.

'We want to see Chief Johnson. Tell him it's

Sonny and Joe, we have an appointment by 4.30 p.m.,' Sonny said as the glass went down.

'OK sir, let me just confirm.'

Some minutes later, the gates were opened and they drove inside. The house was simply superb. Nothing too big, just a storey building but it was breathtaking. French windows opened out in the balcony and the front lawn was lined up with exotic flowers. It was the sort of place one could just relax completely oblivious of the outside world. They pressed the doorbell and almost immediately a servant opened the door.

'Mr Sonny and Mr Joe?'

'Correct.' They nodded.

The servant opened the door wider and they stepped inside the house. Every part of the house radiated opulence.

'This way please.' The servant took them upstairs and right there on the balcony, Chief KK Johnson was relaxing comfortably on a lounge chair.

The balcony was spacious with four lounge chairs and two tables. KK Johnson kept his drink on the side table and went towards his visitors in capable strides. He stopped just in front of them and gazed as if he was inspecting. Then slowly, his mouth quaked in a smile.

'Sit down.'

KK was a very extraordinary human being; Joe thought as he faced the KK Johnson he had heard so much about. He turned out to be much younger than he had imagined. He guessed he might be in his early forties. His grey hair wasn't much and he looked very strong and capable.

Joe had prepared himself for a tirade of long angry speech from KK Johnson but the man didn't look ready for any scolding speech. He looked quite relaxed and unperturbed. KK Johnson took a cigarette and offered to Sonny who took one and lighted. He didn't offer Joe the cigarette.

'I know you don't smoke so what's the use?' he told Joe as he dropped the packet on the side stool. Joe knew KK had a file on every Master in Lagos. He got daily reports; Joe knew that, so he wasn't really surprised at KK's words.

'Why did I call you?' KK asked Sonny and Joe. Joe's sixth sense told him that this was a test. KK Johnson was cunning, Joe could sense it, and so he didn't reply.

KK was studying both of them intently. The little question he asked almost took Sonny off balance. KK was disappointed. Joe was much more composed and was looking at him squarely on the face.

'Sonny? Joe?' KK Johnson raised an eyebrow waiting for an answer.

Sonny spoke first, 'To reprimand us sir, but it

was barely our fault'. Joe flashed Sonny a scowling look.

'OK!' KK Johnson said in his slow drawl. He had a way of speaking, slow but in a peremptory manner. His shrewd eyes, which escaped nothing, studied Joe again. From what he had seen so far, he liked Joe and might use him for the task ahead. The task that would last until maybe twenty years' time and then maybe... well until then. Being a double agent can be highly dangerous.

Joe wondered if he had done anything wrong because of the way KK Johnson was studying him. But nevertheless he remained calm and expressionless despite the battle going on within him. Sonny was furious and confused; he would have walked out on KK if he had been in a position to do so. KK Johnson cleared his throat as an indication that he wanted to speak.

'I called you,' he began slowly, 'not to reprimand you. In fact, that was the last thing on my mind. We lost a very huge amount of money, but it was barely your fault.' He looked at them to emphasize his point. His shrewd eyes did not fail to register the relief clearly expressed on their faces. 'But I believe you people could do better. I believe in perfection and you both know that. Every Master should always tend towards perfection in every duty assigned to him, I keep telling them.' He paused to take a sip of his drink, then gently placed it back on the side table. He was in no hurry. He continued, 'your boys were too careless but then, if you had inculcated fear in them, they would have been more careful. I don't want a repeat.'

Sonny shifted uncomfortably on his chair. He envied Joe who sat still like a statue. Sonny wondered why he called them. *If not to reprimand us, then why?* As if he read his thoughts, KK answered Sonny's silent question.

'I called you here to see you. To know you. I have heard how hardworking the two of you have been, especially Joe who just finished his probation. Tell me Joe have you made plans about who would replace you when you retire? About the person that would *sit for you* as we say it?'

'My wife had a baby girl a month after my probation. She would sit for me in the next twenty-one years.'

'Better train her to be very close to you. Train her up to think like a Master. You know what I mean.'

Some minutes later they were on their way home. Just thirty minutes after Joe had reached home, he had a call from KK Johnson, he would like to see him the next day. 'Between you and I, we have to talk business,' KK had said. The call was snappy.

*   *   *   *   *   *   *   *

'So you see?' KK Johnson was pacing up and down his study. You have to spy on those bastards. I know they are a tough set of people and the job is highly risky, but your pay would be worth it. I don't want this organization to fall again. You know it was the most powerful in Nigeria before the civil war. They were really Masters of the Underworld in every sense of the word, before it mysteriously crumbled during the civil war.

'How did you manage to revive it in so short a time?'

'You'll do the job for me, for the Masters, won't you?' KK asked, ignoring Joe's question.

'Why me? I can't do it single-handed. Sonny would be a good partner.'

'I know why I chose you,' he cut in. 'I know you just finished your probation period but Sonny is an old member; Sonny is not fit for the job and I can't bring myself to trust him one bit.'

'Anyway, I might consider him if the need arises but you shouldn't, you must not mention this to anyone, not even Sonny. It is a very long contract, twenty years. That's the more reason why I insist you do it. You are the youngest person who is capable of doing it. The job shouldn't be difficult for an intelligent man like you.' He chuckled irritably as he came closer to Joe and began in a husky voice. His eyes were boring into Joe's.

'This assignment puts this society in your hands ... to build or to destroy, but you dare not attempt the latter. You dare not drive a single nail into our coffin. You have to use every fibre of your intelligence and don't let anyone or anything intimidate you. The Vikings want to retrieve our power from us, but we will prove our invincibility. They will do anything to get it.' His voice was mellow as he continued 'They can use you, Joe. As a matter of fact, I am supposed to do this task but it is a full time affair. I can't do it for reasons best known to me and remember, perfection.' He lighted another cigarette and resumed his pacing. Joe who had kept mute asked him one of the questions that had been nagging in his head.

'Why do you trust me sir?'

KK turned from the window to face Joe, a slow smile forming on his lips. 'I hope I can trust you,' he said casually over his shoulders as he went to the desk, picked a file marked 'top secret' in red letters, and thrust it on Joe's laps.

'Open the first page and put down your signature in the right place. I have signed mine as you can see.' He picked up another similar file 'Here is my own copy. You have to sign both now, and please read those papers carefully. Inside that file is everything about the task. Em... I hope your safe is very safe. Anybody that gets hold of this file can get anything from the Masters. They can use it to blackmail us into anything because what we are about to do, is against the rules of the Underworld. It is illegal. The rule was made during the Nigerian Underworld Conference a couple of years ago. No spying. If they ever find out, this society is gone, and that is exactly what the Vikings want.'

'Then let us just forget the whole idea,' Joe suggested. KK shook his head.

'Don't chicken out, Joe. This is the only way to preserve the power we have. The end will justify the means. Can't you see?' he gestured impatiently with his hands.

'I can't see!' Joe returned vehemently, but KK continued, ignoring Joe's outburst.

'The Vikings are bent on destroying us. They don't care how long it is going to take them and that is why they planned a twenty-year strategy, they want to use slow poison. I don't know how they would do it, I don't know their moves and that is why I need you to do this job.'

Joe's spirit almost quailed at the dangers ahead. He would be living in constant fear.

'It is too late to back out, Joe,' KK said as he came closer and looked down at the files. 'Sign them. Now.' It was an imperative order.

4

PEARL

Lagos, 1990

Pearl grew up to be a very beautiful and highly precious girl. Her earliest memories were of a loving daddy who showered her with gifts and attention, of a loving mother, though not as loving as daddy. Her mum was closer to Chidi. Uncle KK who adores her and who also spoilt her with gifts and attention, second to her dad.

Sometimes her dad took her with him on business trips, Nigeria and abroad. She enjoyed those trips a lot. Her dad took her with him almost everywhere he went, but the place Pearl loved most was her uncle KK's house. Uncle KK would tell her stories of great heroes and he would teach her how to play cards. He always had time for her. She always liked going there whenever Andrew,

KK's son was not around. Andrew was much bigger than Pearl and much older too, he was seven years older and he was a bully. Pearl knew he hated her or maybe envied her. He would always tell Pearl that her eyes were too big for her. He would call her froggie whenever uncle KK went out. Sometimes he would pinch her, but Pearl never reported to her dad or to uncle KK. She could remember when Andrew's mummy died, the sad look in Andrew's face, his red swollen face and uncle KK's grim face. She was killed in a car accident.

Also indelible in her mind were his daddy's arms and shoulders wrapped up in a bandage. Her daddy's pale face as he lay lackadaisically like a piece of log, on the hospital bed. Her daddy was shot by unknown thieves; her mum had told her. That was just a couple of years ago.

Pearl always had that cool and confident look and many people classified her as reserved. She had few friends. She attended one of the best private secondary schools in Lagos. Their driver took her to and from school each day. Chioma was a very good friend of hers. They were classmates.

Pearl's dad had warned her to be careful about how she mixed up at school, to be careful about the friends she made. She had chosen Chioma because she could sense they had many things in common, Chioma was nice, hardworking in school and she had a confident aura about her. They were called twins because they were always together. Chioma was from a very wealthy family just like Pearl and she was the only girl.

It was break time and they were leaning on the veranda in front of their classroom, biting away their snacks while idly watching what was happening below, school children playing, bullying.

'My dad keeps on asking of you, Pearl. You know I talk a lot about my friends.'

'And what do you talk about me?'

'Everything I know. He said I should tell him all that I know about you and your dad. I didn't know much and he said I should ask you.'

'Why is he so interested?' Pearl took a bite of her sandwich.

'Curiosity. Pearl what does your dad do, I mean his business?'

'He is into import-export business. When I was a kid, he took me with him to most of his business trips,' Pearl said, her face lighting up in reminiscence. 'What of your dad?'

'There is no business he is not into, name it … hotels and catering, crude oil, he has chains of supermarkets scattered throughout Nigeria,' she slightly raised her hands in a simple gesture, 'just everything.' Pearl laughed.

'What is so funny?' Chioma asked as she looked down. 'Oh! You're laughing at your brother.'

'Chidi!' Pearl called out. Chidi looked up and with his hands, he shed the sun from his eyes. He smiled and gave Pearl a thumb-up sign, which Pearl returned. There was a girl by his side.

'Is that his girlfriend?' Chioma asked. Pearl nodded.

'She is in class five, next month Chidi would graduate and she will miss him a lot.'

'What is Chidi going to study in the University?'

'Accountancy. And you, when we graduate in the next couple of years, what would you study in the university?' Pearl asked.

'Law. I would like to be a lawyer. My dad said I would practice abroad, isn't that wonderful. What of you Pearl, what would you study in the university.'

'Maybe I would be a doctor. I will study medicine,' she shrugged 'anyway we still have a couple of years to go.'

*   *   *   *   *   *   *   *

Two years later....

It was 8.30 p.m. Joe stepped out to the streets

and hailed down a taxi. He must be very careful, extra careful.

'El Casino,' he told the driver as the taxi sped off into the warm night. Joe wore a grey T-shirt and black shorts. He had on his feet, black sneakers. He dressed casually, ordinarily. Nobody would ever guess he was a millionaire. Nobody would look twice at him when it comes to his present attire, but when it comes to his face and body build, people would never stop staring. Joe was simply handsome. He didn't want to be noticed, especially now, especially at El Casino.

The taxi screeched to a halt. Joe came out and handed the taxi driver a wad of notes. The taxi driver was all smiles as he thanked him and sped away. The brightly coloured lights from the signpost in front of the building welcomed Joe. This was a joint for gamblers.

Joe went to the bar and ordered gin and tonic. He perched on the stool and watched his surroundings while sipping his drink at intervals. His palms were sweating, he was nervous. He looked at his watch; SK Obi was ten minutes late. Joe wondered whether he would turn up. He was anxious to hear what he had to say. He had called Joe earlier and he said he had some urgent matters to discuss with him. Joe knew they had found out about him, and his sixth sense told him that Vikings wanted to use him. He didn't inform

KK Johnson about the call.

Joe was armed. He had a pistol underneath his shirt and he was prepared just in case SK Obi tried anything silly, but he knew he wouldn't. The Vikings needed him and he had to be alive to help them. But Joe had made up his mind, he wasn't going to help the Vikings neither was he going to help the Masters. He would use slow poison to dissolve both, but the problem was how to start. He was playing with fire, but he was set to protect his daughter's future. Pearl would never be a Master of the Underworld.

A heavyset man in his fifties occupied the stool next to Joe. He ordered martini and looked at Joe. He fit the description. 'SK Obi' he said.

Joe turned slowly and observed the SK Obi he had heard so much about. He was the KK of the Vikings. Joe thought wryly. SK was wearing a traditional attire. He didn't look out of place. Some customers here wore traditional outfits. He wore a gold wristwatch and the fragrance from his expensive cologne was strong. The man didn't have enough stuff in the head. He could have made himself inconspicuous, Joe thought. He noticed that SK Obi's hand was still outstretched, waiting for him.

'Joe Mbakwe.' The two men shook hands.

'We can't talk here, too noisy,' SK said.

'I think I noticed a restaurant across the street,'

Joe said draining his glass.

The restaurant was small and cosy. It had few people and one could talk in privacy. They chose a corner table at the far end of the restaurant. The light was dim. It was just what Joe wanted. The waiter came and they ordered drinks.

'I understand you're a Master. I've had you watched for more than ten years while you've been trying to dig out every information you could about Vikings.' He stopped as the waiter returned with the drinks. When the waiter had gone, he continued.

'Initially, we mistook you for a snoopy policeman or from Investigation Bureau, later we found out you were a Master. We tried to eliminate you but you just escaped with only bullet wounds. It was later that the idea struck me, the idea that you might help us to retrieve our power back from the Masters. To get our documents for us. You know something Mr. Mbakwe, what you are doing is against the rules of the NUC.' Joe still kept mute. He poured his malt drink into the glass and sipped. SK Obi continued, not touching his drink.

'It is against the rules and the Masters would be penalized seriously or worse still, dissolved but,' he slightly raised his hands. 'I don't want that. I want KK Johnson to know they are playing with fire. I want to get hold of the documents and set it ablaze in KK Johnson's presence, and his firm?' he laughed. 'I'll make sure it crumbles like a pack of cards. So,' his face was serious as he continued, 'Name the price. You're getting the documents for us not only the documents, you'll have to give us any information that would be useful to us.' He poured a decent amount of martini, took out a cigarette and lighted. He didn't offer Joe and Joe wondered whether he also knew that he didn't smoke.

'I'm not for sale,' Joe said.

'I know,' SK returned flippantly.

'That would be too risky for me.'

'You'll get protection, twenty-four hours.'

'I love my privacy.'

'But you've never had privacy.'

Joe thought about that and he knew it was true. Very true. Ever since he became a Master, he never had privacy. He sighed.

'How much naira?' SK Obi said. Joe laughed, throwing back his head.

'I'll think about it for three million dollars,' Joe said. He drained his glass as a signal that the talk was over. SK Obi understood. He nodded. He was a patient man. He would wait. He would watch.

'If you would spare a few minutes, I want you to listen to a short story that might interest you,' SK Obi said relaxing on his chair. He was in no hurry. 'I'm not telling you this story to gain favour from you,' he paused to let his words sink in. He had caught Joe's attention. 'I just think it might help you if you are doing the job for us.' He put the cigarette stub in the ashtray and folded his arms on the table, leaning closer.

'Just before the civil war, Masters of the Underworld had a serious clash with Mafia. You know Mafia was much more powerful and during that period too, the Masters were almost fished out by the federal government. They were in a deadlock. So in order to avoid Mafia striking and to avoid the latter too, they changed their name to Vikings. Before the war, there was nothing like Vikings. People still think the Masters collapsed, but I'm telling you they merely changed their name. But,' he raised a finger to emphasize, 'one thing is that their change of name brought about a drastic downfall in their power. But we've worked so hard in the past few years and we'll soon be much more powerful than we were before the civil war.'

'And the present Masters?' Joe couldn't help asking.

'Is fake. A man materialized out of nowhere, worked in collaboration with an unfaithful Viking, faked our most important documents and started an organization ...the present Masters of the Underworld. The Organization became very powerful because of the name... people thought it was the same Masters of the Underworld which terrorized the top men of Nigeria before the war.'

'How did you find out all these things?'

'It's a long story but I found out seventeen years ago and since then we've been scheming to get what belongs to us …the documents and the name. Without the fake docs, Masters would just crumble like a pack of cards. They'll lose everything. They'll lose their power.'

'And your story is genuine?'

'I can prove, it.'

'Then do.'

'It will cost you.'

'What's the price?'

'It is not for sale. Meanwhile, contact me whenever you have something positive for us… and Mr. Mbakwe,' he said as he got up, 'Just know how to talk, your mouth could get you killed.' He left without a backward glance, walking casually and with ease.

Joe looked at his watch, the light was dim but he could make out what the time was. It was twelve minutes past ten. He signalled the waiter and ordered another bottle of malt. There are things he had to sort out in his head; there are plans he had to make.

It was 10.35 p.m. when Joe settled the waiter and went out of the restaurant. Hands in pockets, he sauntered down the street. All of a sudden he was covered with goose pimples despite the warm weather. He had this premonition that something terrible was going to happen. He had this uncomfortable feeling that he was being followed. He had been watched since he became a Master and he was used to it, but this was different. He had avoided being followed to El Casino, that was why he had used a cab, that was why he had fixed the appointment in the night, he sighed. He was imagining things. He looked behind him but didn't see anything suspicious. He flagged down a cab and went home. He stopped at the street corner and then jogged down to his house. Anybody would think he just went for jogging.

He opened the front door and went inside the sitting room. He flopped down on a sofa and just then noticed the other person in the sofa at the other side of the room. It was Pearl. He knew she had been waiting for him and maybe fell asleep. He removed his sneakers, went over to Pearl and nudged her a little. She woke up.

'Dad, don't tell me you've been jogging for the past...' she looked at the clock on the wall, 'three hours. I was worried,' she shrugged. 'I don't want you to get shot again. It's not an experience anybody would like.' Joe grinned.

'So you were waiting. Where's Marina?'

'Mum's asleep.'

'And Chidi?'

'Sleeping.'

'Then we had better go and get our own sleep. Did anybody call while I was away?'

'Yes. Uncle KK called. I told him you went jogging, an hour or so later, he called again, I told him you weren't back. He said he wants to see you first thing tomorrow morning. Anyway, I'm going over there for the weekend,' she yawned. 'I'd better go to bed. Goodnight dad.' She went over to the refrigerator and drank a glass of water. It was a habit.

'Goodnight, dear. Sleep tight,' Joe said as he watched Pearl climb the stairs. He watched his daughter. He truly loved Pearl and wished he were not a Master. His daughter wouldn't find it funny if she found out he was an unscrupulous daddy, Marina wouldn't find it funny too and Chidi, no. He stifled a soul-wrenching sob, and he would do anything in his power to destroy the Masters without implicating himself or his family. His daughter would never be a Master.

'Daddy!' he turned sharply, Pearl was on the staircase 'what is it, something's worrying you?'

'Pearl, go and sleep'

'The phone in your study is ringing.'

'Let it ring Pearl, I'm going straight to bed.' He wearily climbed the stairs.

5

7.00 a.m. Joe kissed Marina goodbye as he carried his small suitcase out to the waiting car. It was a grey Pathfinder. Joe loved the car. He dismissed the driver; he loved driving himself when he used the Pathfinder. He started the engine and headed towards KK Johnson's house. He wondered what the man was up to.

'We are in a fix,' KK Johnson said as soon as Joe entered his office.

'We?'

'Masters of the Underworld, KK and Co. Well there's nothing that cannot be worked out. My boys uncovered a terrifying tale of betrayal. I'm really disappointed, Joe,' Joe stiffened. His schemes have already been discovered. KK continued. 'Tell me everything you know about Sonny's deal with the Mafia.'

'Mafia?' Joe said unbelievably. 'If anything exists between Sonny and the Mafia, I know nothing about it.'

'Joe you don't expect me to believe that. You are real close to Sonny, family friends, and business associate. You don't have to be a private investigator to know that such deal exists. Sonny has been trying to sell us to Mafia that is all I can tell you as of now. I want you to find out more about the deal. You are in the position to do that without much trouble. It is an order, if you don't then you become a traitor.' KK Johnson stood up and casually paced about.

'About your job, any information about Vikings.'

'No.'

'Then what the hell have you been doing. You think we paid you millions just to gum your buttocks on a seat and take everything nonchalantly. You haven't gotten any real, I mean REAL information and that is exactly why I hired you to carry out the task....'

The week that followed was hellish for Joe. His dilemma was worse. Sonny was quite oblivious of what was happening. Joe found out that there really was a deal between Mafians and Sonny. Sonny was a traitor, he was a good friend and Joe was torn. However, he still kept his mouth shut despite the tirade of long angry speech from KK Johnson.

A month later Sonny was found dead in his car

that was parked on the Lagos - Badagry expressway. It looked like heart attack while driving. Joe had no doubts KK Johnson had struck. The Mafia had no doubts KK Johnson had struck.

KK's boys had ambushed Sonny as he drove towards Badagry on an official duty. They had covered his face with a polythene bag, suffocated him and left, leaving no trace, not a single shred of evidence for the police.

Joe knew Sonny would get killed sooner or later; nobody plays with the Masters and gets away with it. He had kept all his affairs with Vikings at a standstill ever since Sonny died. The impact of what he had been doing hit him. He was terrified but it was something he had to do. He had to destroy the Masters.

Kate wept uncontrollably when she heard the news of her husband's death, their twenty-one-year-old son, Bayo tried so hard to console her mum but he didn't do much of a work.

A week later, all the Masters in Lagos together with their families paid their last respects to Sonny Adele. The church was full and the atmosphere was solemn. Joe's eyes watered, just like Marina's and many others.

In the afternoon, Joe who had been taking a nap on the sofa was awakened by the continuous shrill of the phone. He swore under his breath as he picked up the receiver. It was from Joint Admissions and Matriculation Board. The results of the Joint Matriculation Examination were out, Pearl Mbakwe's result was marvellous and they wondered whether Joe still wanted them to cancel his daughter's results. Just like they did the first one last year. Joe had paid them a heavy amount of money to do it.

'Go on, cancel it,' Joe said authoritatively into the receiver. He dropped the receiver, and stretched himself.

It was Saturday afternoon. The house was quiet. The phone rang again. It was Chidi calling from school. Just as he graduated from secondary school, he had secured admission at the University of Lagos to study accountancy.

'Chidi how are you?'

'I'm fine dad.'

'And School? When is the semester ending?'

'Next month. Is mum there?'

'Upstairs.'

'And Pearl?'The Joint matric Result would be out next week I'll check hers.'

'Please do.'

'Dad something weird is going on here, I want to discuss it with you. It scares me.'

'Weird?'

'Yes. I'll be home tomorrow.' And Joe was kept in suspense for twenty-four hours.

49

Joe was having lunch with Marina and Pearl. It was a sunny Sunday. The conversation around the table was next to none. They all concentrated on their food. Fried rice with roast turkey. Marina hated eating in silence. She knew that Joe was simply not in the mood for any chitchat.

'So how was the weekend with your uncle?' she asked Pearl.

Pearl grimaced 'Very boring. Uncle KK was so busy, thundering to his employees on the phone 'find out!' or 'I want 24 hours surveillance!' or 'nail him!' then there were the curses, I never knew uncle KK could use bad language.'

'Too bad,' Marina commented. Joe was listening to the conversation with rapt attention. An idea formed in his head. He could tell his secrets to his family, they would all help in one way or the other to dissolve the Masters. Pearl could get information from KK....

'Just in time for lunch!' Chidi said as he busted into the dining room.

'No you're late, you ain't getting even the crumbs!' Pearl said jokingly.

'Don't mind her,' Marina said laughing. 'I'll get yours.'

After the lunch, Marina and Pearl went for a swim while Joe called Chidi upstairs to his study. Joe sat at the edge of the table, one leg on the floor and the other swinging. He leaned on one elbow. He was ready to hear the weird story. Chidi was pacing slowly.

'Dad is anyone blackmailing you?'

Joe stopped the swinging. 'What makes you think that I'm being blackmailed?'

'Are you in some kind of trouble?'

Joe shrugged 'Hit the nail, Chidi.'

'They said I should warn you,' Chidi said stopping to look at his dad.

'Who?'

'I don't know. They didn't tell me.'

'I don't understand,' Chidi sat on the chair.

'Dad I'm being followed at school. I don't know, but I think we have very dangerous enemies on our tracks. They keep following me at school, calling my apartment and when I pick up the phone a hoarse voice tells me to warn my dad, before I ask who's on the line, he would drop.' There was a tense silence.

'When did it start?' Joe asked.

'They've been following me for a month and a few days at least that was when I noticed, and the phone calls started just last week.'

'Mmm... I have to think, Chidi. There are things I have to sort out, then we'd have a long talk....'

Chidi got up. 'Whatever you have to do, be fast about it, those people sound deadly dad, and I'd like to have the privacy of not being followed.'

'Don't worry about that.'

'Is there anything I can do to help?'

'I'll call you whenever I need your help. Thanks Chidi.'

When Chidi had gone, Joe paced the length of his study thinking hard. He suspected SK Obi, Joe hadn't contacted him since that day in El Casino... but what if KK Johnson had gotten information about his meeting with SK Obi and was trying to scare Joe? Joe hurried downstairs to call Chidi, a thought occurring to him.

'Chidi!' he called out. He found him at the pool with Marina and Pearl.

When they reached the house Joe told him 'Chidi next time he calls, tell him you've warned me, that I said he should fix a date, I want to talk to him or it would be better if we met. That's all.' He casually slapped his son at the back. 'You can go back to the pool and have fun. I'll join you people in a minute.'

*   *   *   *   *   *   *   *

'Chioma when is the semester ending?'

'Next month, why?'

'You need to take a break from your studies. Why don't you spend some time in my suite at De Plaza resort, and please invite your friend, Pearl.'

'Oh dad! You're so nice, that was so thoughtful

of you. And Pearl would be so glad to come.' Chioma said as she embraced her dad. 'At least I'll take a break from school stress. Law is a course full of stress.'

'When are you planning to go?'

'In two days time, on Friday.'

SK Obi nodded. Two days is enough time to make other arrangements that is if the girl would accept the invitation.

'Do you think Pearl would accept the invitation?' SK asked his daughter. He went to the bar at the far end of the sitting room and mixed a drink for himself.

'Why not? We haven't seen each other for the past couple of years, ever since we graduated from secondary school. So it is very likely, most likely she would accept.'

'So the two of you haven't been in touch.'

'Yes. But I see her brother, Chidi in School at times.'

'Her brother is in University of Lagos?'

'Yeah. Third year accountancy'

'And Pearl?'

'Her Joint Matric. Exams were cancelled twice. It is quite a pity. I have a very curious daddy.'

Thursday morning dawned bright and gay. It was a beautiful day and Joe wished he could just play truant at work for just this once. But he had to go.

There wasn't much work in the office, both on the legitimate and illegitimate sides. The only task on the legitimate side was clearing of their goods in the wharf. They were electronic wares from Japan, and many other goods. They would be kept in the warehouse until they are sold. Ten minutes past twelve Joe's intercom buzzed.

'A call from Chidi Mbakwe,' his secretary said.

'My son! I'd take the call,' Joe said dropping the pen he was using on the table.

'Dad come over, he'll call again by 1.00 p.m.'

'I'll be right there. Chidi how are you?'

'Fine.'

Twelve-thirty Joe was already at Chidi's apartment in the school. He looked around him.

'Mmm... nice place you've got here. When I was in the university I only dreamt of a place like this, but never saw it. You're very lucky Chidi.'

The soft baritone voice of Luther Vandross filled the room as Chidi slid in the disc. He started dancing.

'Is that the latest style?' Joe asked. Chidi nodded.

'In our time it used to be like this,' Joe demonstrated sending Chidi to fits of laughter. Joe did a twist that sent him doubling up in pain.

'Ouch! Old age is catching up on me, I used to be a very flexible guy,' he removed his jacket and hung it on the chair, then threw himself on the couch. His eyes caught the ashtray on the side stool almost full of cigarette stumps and ash.

'Don't tell me you smoke Chidi'

'Yeah I do dad, occasionally.'

Joe shrugged 'suit yourself but please don't go for dope.'

The phone rang and the two pairs of eyes stared at the object as if it was some kind of an alien. Then Joe picked the receiver.

'Hello.... Yeah could you call back in an hour's time, he's not around.' He dropped it and swore silently under his breath.

'I almost got the jitters,' he said to Chidi.

'Who was that?'

'She said her name was Jenny.'

'My girlfriend.'

'You never told me about her.'

'Mum knows and Pearl too, since secondary school.'

'Wow! I'd like to meet her.'

The phone rang again. Joe picked the receiver with hands that shook slightly.

'Yeah,' Joe said trying to sound casual and at ease.

'Joe Mbakwe we have to meet…, it is high time we met.'

'Who are you?'

'I am a Mafian.'

'I don't think I have anything....'

'That is a silly thing to say. Meet me where you met SK Obi ...at that little restaurant. I'll be there by eight.' And he dropped.

Joe sighed and slowly dropped his receiver.

'Did he say his name?' Chidi was hyper-curious.

'Didn't. But it was from the Mafia.'

Chidi gaped at his dad and shook his head.

'Mafia? What business do you have with them?'

'Chidi there are lots of things you don't know. I was trapped in a web twenty-one years ago and I'm trying escape. I'm in a mix up with three notorious organizations; the Masters, Vikings and now the Mafia.'

'I don't understand.'

'Chidi sit down, it's high time I told you what I've been going through since 1972, since my employment at KK and Co import and export, swear you'll keep it a secret even to Marina and Pearl, we'll tell them later but not yet.'

'I swear,' Chidi said, mockingly raising up his palms.

And Joe narrated to his son, the story of his life since 1972.

Chidi whistled softly 'Incredible,' he said 'we have to act fast dad, Pearl will soon be twenty and the Masters expect her to marry at twenty years to take over at twenty-one. It means you have only a year to destroy the Masters. Pearl would never be a Master.'

'And now I wonder what the hell Mafians want from me,' Joe said. Hands in pocket, he wandered to the window and stood looking out with unseeing eyes.

'You have to meet them to hear what they have to say, but dad be very careful, those sets of guys don't flinch at the sight of blood. They might even want to use you to get at Masters.'

'They've been watching me. How the hell did they know I met SK Obi and even where I met him?'

'Dammit dad!' Chidi swore as he got up and paced about the room. 'I wish I could help. You'll get killed if KK Johnson finds out.'

'Just like Sonny,' there was a tense silence. 'I'll be extra careful this time,' Joe sighed.

'I have an idea'

Ten minutes to eight, Chidi walked casually into the dimly lit restaurant. The place was packed up with people and smoke filled up the place. Luckily for him he found a table and signalled the waiter. He wanted just Coca-Cola. He brought out a packet of Dunhill and slid out a stick. He lighted it, relaxed back in his chair, and looked around him. Surely they would recognise him. Maybe they are not yet here. There was a little commotion at the far end of the restaurant, a drunken man was shouting at the waiter to bring another round of vodka and threatening to destroy things if his request was not granted.

'Go home to your wife, silly drunkard!' The small-framed waiter shouted back as two bouncers carried the drunken man away with little or no difficulty. The drunken man belched and shouted 'Get your hands off me!'

A waiter brought the Coca Cola and Chidi paid, giving him a generous tip. Just as the waiter went, a man in his late twenties or early thirties with roughly chiselled features, sat opposite Chidi. He was wearing an almost oversized but expensive suit. He was neatly dressed.

'You are not Joe.'

'I know. Follow me and you'll meet him.' Chidi stood up and left the unopened bottle of Coca Cola. He walked out of the restaurant into the fresh night air, entered his car, a grey Honda Prelude and sped off. He knew the Mafian was following.

Joe saw them from the window. Chidi got out of the car, locked it and walked towards the house after glancing casually down on the street. A few minutes later a black Mercedes parked a few yards away from the grey Honda. A man in suit came out and followed Chidi. He was in no hurry. Chidi entered before him.

'He's coming.' He told Joe as he went inside the inner room just then there was a light knock on the door.

'Come in.'

The man entered the apartment and nodded slightly in appraisal as he looked around him. Hands in pocket he went over to the wall, looked at the posters and turned to Joe. 'Used to have a place like this when I was a student.' The man looked completely at ease and Joe was furious.

'What do you want?' Joe asked in a flat tone. The man brought out a small tape recorder and pressed a button. Joe's conversation with SK Obi filled the room. It was very clear, and anybody would recognise his voice. He stopped the tape after some time.

'Where did you get that?' Joe asked. The man ignored his question and brought out a sheet of paper. It was the plan of a house.

'This is KK and Co. I want you to plant explosives at those points marked 'x', and I want it done in three days time. It is either that or,' he raised the tape 'KK gets this, the explosives are waiting at 12 Lawal Street.' He handed Joe a key. Hands in pocket he went towards the door.

'Remember, three days time.' And he left, slowly closing the door.

6

Joe Mbakwe knocked again on Pearl's bedroom door.

'You have a phone call.' Pearl opened the door and rubbed sleepy eyes.

'Maybe I'll tell her you are having your siesta,' Joe suggested as he turned to go. 'It's Chioma, your former classmate you told me about. I hope you didn't get too close to her, some friends might turn out to be your foes.'

'Hey! Chioma! I'll speak with her of course,' she said, ignoring Joe's last statement. She ran down the stairs to the sitting room and took the receiver.

'Chioma! Is that really you?.

... so you're calling from your house.

... holidays?.... OK.

... I'd love to come but... well I'll call you, what is the number?... of course.

... could you believe it has been two years since we left school and that was the last time I heard from you... OK.'

She dropped the receiver and flopped down on the nearest sofa. Chioma had invited her to spend some days with her at De Plaza Resort, Enugu. Chioma's dad had suggested a break from her studies, and had given her his private suite there, Pearl mentioned it to her dad.

'Don't even consider it Pearl, anything can happen to you.'

'But I need a break, I'm getting bored here and moreover, I haven't seen Chioma for two years, dad there's something you don't seem to understand and that is the fact that I am no longer a kid. I... I just want to go out and be on my own for once in my life, mix up with people, see the world on my own... if you really love me I don't see any reason why I can't go....'

'OK! OK! You can go,' Joe waved impatiently with a hand. Pearl heaved a sigh of relief 'but on one condition. You must go with your bodyguard.'

After some moments, Pearl sighed resolutely. 'OK. That's fair enough.'

*　　*　　*　　*　　*　　*　　*　　*

'Pearl are you sure you would be alright, you are being unnecessarily stubborn, let the driver take you....'

'No dad, let me just use a taxi for once in my life. Let me do something on my own just for once,' Pearl almost retorted. Marina who was standing close to Joe, nodded in silent agreement. Her daughter was growing up.

Joe looked at his daughter's seriously pleading face as she argued with him.

'Pearl, when did this spirit of independence get into you? Anyway have it your way, but don't ever go anywhere without your bodyguard, you hear me?'

'OK dad. Mum bye!' she entered the waiting taxi and her bodyguard followed suit.

'Take care!' Marina said as the taxi sped off.

'We would stop at the Apex transport terminal,' Pearl instructed the driver as she settled back on the back seat and let her thoughts wonder. She wished she would find a way to bribe her bodyguard. For once in her life, she wanted to be like others, to have a taste of freedom.

When they reached the station, the bus heading to Enugu was getting ready to set off. They were very lucky to get seats. Ten minutes later the bus set off. Pearl heaved a sigh of relief as she settled more comfortably on the seat. This was her first time travelling on a bus. It was more fun. Her dad had insisted she went by flight, but she had refused. She hoped she would enjoy her short stay at Enugu. She closed her eyes and let the steady hum of the bus send her to a deep slumber.

Pearl woke up with a start and wondered how long she had slept. She looked around her, something she had not really done since she entered the bus. She had been sleeping on and off; she hadn't really looked around her.

The bus was full and each passenger seemed to be occupied with their own thoughts, however, some of them were chatting among themselves. There were three others in her row apart from her bodyguard, two young girls around the same age as herself or a bit older and a man who she guessed must be around the same age as her father. The two girls chatted excitedly about Enugu and how they were going to spend their holiday.

'Isn't it great to lodge in De Plaza resort for a whole week wow! I just can't wait to reach Enugu and wallow in the luxury!' The darker one was less excited or rather showed less excitement.

'Did I hear you say De Plaza?' Pearl asked the younger one ignoring the scowling look her bodyguard flashed at her, 'I'm going there too, I'm staying for a few days.'

'Oh that is great!' replied the fair girl 'I'm Linda and this is my cousin Ify.'

'I'm Pearl.'

'Have you ever been to De Plaza? Heard it is such a nice place.'

'I've never been there but I've heard so much about it'

Pearl joined in their conversation and they talked through the whole journey. They stopped at a filling station somewhere along the way and the passengers refreshed themselves. Fifteen minutes later they were on the road again. The steady hum of the bus sent most of the passengers asleep.

'Guess where we are?' Ify said excitedly, following her gaze, Pearl saw the sign just before they sped past it. It read 'Welcome to Enugu State' and underneath in small letters 'the coal city'

'So we are really in Enugu, I haven't been aware of the time' Pearl said as she briefly looked at her watch. She exclaimed 'It is four o'clock, can you believe we've been on the road for the past eight hours!'

'Yes and your brother has been sleeping for the past three hours,' chipped in Linda.

'He's not my brother.'

'Oh! Your boyfriend?'

'God! No, my bodyguard,' replied Pearl who didn't miss the looks the two cousins exchanged.

'My dad insisted,' she shrugged. Linda giggled.

'He follows you everywhere?' she asked. 'What a job.'

'I can't help it, I wish I could get him off my back, I'm sick of being followed everywhere.'

'I'll get him off your back if that is what you want, isn't he cute?'

'Oh, he is all yours for the asking!' Pearl said as she glanced discreetly at Sam, her bodyguard to check if he was still sleeping. He was.

De Plaza turned out to be a very big building with a wide entrance at the front. It also had other buildings detached from the main house, Pearl observed as she looked around her. The parking lot was filled with cars and the drive way was lined with exotic palms. The place was simply superb. De Plaza was bustling with life as customers drifted in and out.

They mounted steps that led to the entrance and were welcomed with a nod from the doorman. They went over to the reception. Ify and Linda were staying in room 334, a two-bedroom suite.

'Please could you give me Miss Chioma Obi's room number' Pearl was talking with the lady at the reception.

'Chief Obi's daughter. You are...?'

'Pearl Mbakwe.'

'She is expecting you. You'll find her in room 309,' she smiled. 'The best suite in this resort.

Have a nice stay.'

Pearl knocked lightly and went inside without waiting for an answer. She turned to her bodyguard.

'You stay here, I'll be back.' She went inside the bedroom, leaving Sam in the sitting room, which was small but cosy.

'Chioma is this really you?' Pearl said as she came inside the room. Chioma turned from the wardrobe and screamed in delight, hugging her friend.

'Look at you! How big and healthy.'

Pearl laughed 'Oh! Come off it. I haven't changed much, just added weight.'

'The same old Pearl! You must be tired from your journey, I think a bath and food will do you wonders.'

Pearl smiled wistfully, shaking her head she said 'Chioma you're such a nice fellow!'

Chioma smiled casually as she hung the last dress and closed the wardrobe.

'What are friends for?' she turned. 'Pearl, something is missing,' she observed. 'Don't tell me you have forgotten your travelling bag.'

'Oh! It's in the sitting room, em... I came with my bodyguard, Sam.'

'Bodyguard for what?'

'My dad insisted.'

'Anyway, he can have the second room; thank

God this is a two-bedroom suite. So Pearl how was your trip, you came by flight?'

'No, Apex. I think it is more interesting and I met some friends, they are also staying here....'

The two girls entered the two-bedroom suite and looked around them.

'This is easier than I thought,' one of the girls said flopping down on the bed. 'And this,' she said gesturing towards the whole room.

'Is a bonus,' the other girl completed as she went towards the telephone on the dressing table. She dialled.

'Who are you calling?' the other one asked.

'The boss'

'Hello,' she said into the receiver. 'This is Linda Okeke, the girl is here.... Yes sir.' She dropped the receiver and sighed.

'Let's make a plan,' she said to the other girl.

The sleeper moaned and turned as the early morning sunlight, which filtered through the light curtains, got intense. The shower was on, she could hear the sounds and wondering where she was, she suddenly flew her eyelids open and the events of yesterday all came flooding back to her with a sudden rush. She was in Enugu. She closed her eyes again trying to make out plans for the day.

'Wake up sleepyhead!' It was Chioma, emerging from the bathroom.

'What time is it?' Pearl asked, opening her eyes for the second time. She now looked at her surrounding; the room was well furnished with all the luxuries you can think of. She hadn't noticed much yesterday.

'This place is really nice,' she commented, sitting up in bed.

'Yeah, this is where my dad stays whenever he needs a break.' Chioma looked at the clock on the dressing table 'Past eight for goodness sake!' she exclaimed. 'Get up let's go and get some breakfast.'

Pearl got up and stretched herself. She went to look out from the window. 'Beautiful!' she whispered to herself. 'You've got a wonderful view up here,' she told Chioma. The window overlooked the swimming pool and a few other detached buildings, then part of the tennis lawn. The swimming pool was already crowded and the whole place seemed to be busy.

'It is like everybody in the city is up. Have you seen Sam?'

'Sam?'

'My bodyguard'

Chioma shook her head 'maybe he is not yet

up.'

Pearl grabbed her towel and headed for the shower. 'I'll be ready in ten minutes!' she called out.

'Ten minutes and I'm leaving.'

* * * * * * * *

'Joe, what is worrying you?' Marina asked her husband as they ate their breakfast. 'You were tossing and turning on the bed last night, you didn't sleep. Look at the small bags under your eyes, and see,' she said gesturing towards his plate of food. 'You are not eating. Joe, I have to be a part of whatever is bothering you.'

'You're imagining things.'

'Don't arouse my anger, Joe. Look at you! Do you want to kill yourself?'

'Shut up Marina!' Joe got up and stormed out of the dinning room. He was fully dressed for work. He climbed the stairs, two at a time. *Two more days* was all he kept saying over and over in his mind. He must sneak out all documents that are useful to Vikings before he plants the explosives. He went to his study, fetched his briefcase and hurried out of the house to the waiting car. The bunch of keys was still on the door. He forgot to lock the door to his study.

'Hello!' Pearl waved to Linda and Ify as she passed the swimming pool.

'These are the people I was telling you about,' she said to Chioma. They were heading towards the small restaurant, which was detached from the main building. They had to pass the swimming pool on their way.

'Wait a minute!' Linda called out to Pearl as she came towards them. Pearl introduced her to Chioma and she smiled impatiently 'hi!' as she took Pearl by the hand and led her away.

'Excuse me!' Pearl called over her shoulders to Chioma.

'Pearl where is your bodyguard?' Linda asked once they were alone.

'I haven't seen him maybe he overslept,' Pearl answered nonchalantly.

'You still want him off your back?'

'More than anything else! I don't see any reason why I need a bodyguard.'

'Like you are some kind of a president or something.'

Pearl nodded. 'Exactly.'

'Well,' Linda continued. 'I think I'll get him off your back. He is so cute isn't he? She let out a short laugh. 'Anyway, let me not keep your friend waiting. Em... what is your room number?'

'309.'

'OK. See you some other time.'

'She promised to get Sam off my back, I think she's in love with him.' Pearl said happily to Chioma. They were eating their breakfast in the restaurant.

'Your dad might have a genuine reason for giving you a bodyguard,' Chioma said.

'He is just overprotective. Just tell me one good reason why I shouldn't have my freedom,' she shook her head. 'It is just irritating,' she said with a mouthful of toast.

'Your bodyguard is here.'

Pearl turned her head to see Sam walking furiously towards their table.

'You shouldn't be out without me, anything can happen to you!' he rasped out.

'Just who are you to tell me,' Pearl replied coolly.

'I'll be held responsible if anything happens to you. Your father will just cut off my head.'

'And why should anything happen, Sam? Just what do you think would happen? I didn't tell anybody I was coming to Enugu so I am very, very safe here. Moreover, I don't think I have enemies. Go and enjoy yourself, Sam. Remind me to give you some money for shopping. Have you had breakfast?'

'I'm not sure this is right.' Sam shook his head in a confused manner as he drew his chair closer to the table.

'What is right? Having breakfast?' she laughed. 'Chioma did you hear that?'

'I'm not sure that leaving you alone is right. I don't want to lose my job as well as my head.' The two girls laughed at his comment.

'You are overreacting, Sam. Go and enjoy yourself,' Pearl said sipping her tea.

'OK, OK!' He said with a casual gesture. 'I give up!'

'Oh don't give up!' said a voice from the behind. The three pairs of eyes turned to look at Linda who was standing near them.

'May I join you people, I hate eating alone.'

'You are free to do so,' Pearl replied, motioning her to occupy the only vacant seat left on their table. She glanced at Sam and winked at Pearl as she sat down. She was really dressed to kill and Pearl's eyes didn't fail to register the looks Sam gave her.

Pearl was resting near the swimming pool with Chioma when they saw Linda and Sam as they entered a taxi. Sam was grinning from ear to ear and Linda was saying something to him.

'I don't like how Linda behaves,' Chioma said as the taxi sped off. The twosome in the taxi did not see them.

Pearl shot a questioning glance 'how?'

'Come on Pearl, don't tell me you didn't notice how she was looking at Sam, like a cheap prostitute.' Chioma couldn't hide her disgust. 'But she loves him!' Pearl protested. Chioma let out a short laugh.

'Don't tell me you are that naive, Pearl. That girl is a prostitute believe it or not. Anyway,' she shrugged. 'It doesn't concern me so I had better shut up.'

'Yes, do shut up,' she returned vehemently.

Chioma said coolly, 'Pearl you have changed a lot. You have a big problem, girl,' with that she took her towel and headed towards the main building, to her room.

Pearl slid inside the pool and swam with undue force. She swam to the far end of pool and back again 'Pearl!' she turned to see Ify coming towards the pool. She came out and wrapped herself in the big towel.

'Ify where are you coming from?'

'I just had a long walk. Some of my friends are coming by 6.00 p.m. would you like to go with us to town? You haven't seen the city and I know you've started getting bored.'

'I don't think so.'

'It is OK if you don't want' her face fell 'I... I just thought you would like to experience that freedom of not having a bodyguard with you'

'OK! Six o'clock.'

A satisfactory smile played on Ify's lips. '6.00 p.m.'

'And you are going?' Chioma asked Pearl. She nodded.

'You are being too erratic. If I were you I wouldn't have anything to do with those people... they look fake and I have this premonition that they bring nothing but trouble.'

'Chioma I'll be fine. Keep your premonition to yourself,' Pearl replied as she put on her shoes.

'Just be careful.'

'I'll be fine. I'm going to enjoy myself.'

'Suit yourself.'

7

The grey Pathfinder slid down the lonely street at the outskirts of Ikeja. The driver swerved occasionally to avoid the pot holes that scattered haphazardly along the road. After two turnings by the right he seemed confused, he stopped in front of a small kiosk, wound down his glass and signaled the small boy in the kiosk.

'Good morning sir,' the small boy said as he came towards the car. The driver nodded and wondered whether the boy would be of any help. He decided to try, the boy was not really small, he should be around twelve years.

'Where is Lawal Street?'

'Lawal Street?' the boy repeated and the driver nodded.

'The next street by the left,' the boy said as he openly admired the car. 'Sir, would you like to buy anything?'

The driver shook his head.

'Not even cigarettes?' the boy asked. The

driver ignored the boy's question as he took out two crisp notes from his wallet and handed them to the boy.

'Have it.' The boy took it and the driver drove off. He looked at the rearview mirror and saw the boy still waving excitedly, his face was all smiles.

Joe slowed down a lot as he entered Lawal Street. The feeling of fear and trepidation once again washed through him. His palms were sweating. The Mafian's voice was still clear in his memory. 'I want you to plant explosives at these points marked 'x' and I want it done in three days time. It is either that or....' The blast of a horn brought Joe back to reality and he noticed he was on the wrong lane. He nearly collided with a yellow Volkswagen. Shaking his head to clear his mind, he shouted apologies to the other driver who was showering him with all sorts of abuses in Yoruba language.

Without much difficulty, Joe located number 12. It was a small bungalow, just like others in the street was fenced and had wrought iron gates. Joe stopped the car and got out. He casually looked around him; the street was just like any other street, nothing extraordinary.

Joe pressed the bell beside the gate and waited for an answer. There was none. He pressed it again and again then tried the gate. It was open. He went inside the compound. His eyes took in every part of the compound. It was a small one but neat and well kept. He pressed the doorbell as he reached the front door, waited for a few seconds and just as he raised his hands to press again, he heard someone cough inside. It sounded more like a croak. He heard the shuffling of feet. An elderly woman opened the door. Despite the daylight the woman peered at Joe, her eyes coal black in contrast to her fair wrinkled face.

'Good morning madam,' Joe said.

The woman nodded still looking at Joe with expressionless shrewd eyes. Joe thought he was in the wrong house but he decided to try and, make sure.

'I am Joe Mbakwe,' Joe said, looking at the woman's face to see whether his name would register in her face. It didn't. Her face was still expressionless. Joe continued, 'I was sent to collect some things here.' The woman nodded and Joe felt more comfortable with the broad smile on the woman's face.

'Come in! Oscar traveled yesterday, he said someone would come and pick it in three days time,' the woman rattled on as she led the way down a dim corridor.

'Oscar?' Joe couldn't help asking. The woman turned 'was it not Oscar that sent you? Before Joe could think of any suitable reply, she opened a door that led to a small-overcrowded store. The woman pointed at a medium sized carton on top of an old wooden box. 'There it is,' she said.

Joe lifted the carton. It was a bit heavy. The carton was thoroughly sealed; he didn't try to open it.

'Is that all?' Joe asked. The woman nodded.

Back in the car Joe found a blade and cut open the tapes sealing the carton. On top of the explosives was a piece of paper. He read the instructions clearly stated on the paper. He glanced nervously around, nothing extraordinary was happening. With hands that shook slightly, he picked up one of the explosives and took a close look. He dropped it quietly again, there were six other explosives in the carton. He sighed deeply, put on his sunglasses and started the engine. He would keep the explosives in the basement of his house until two days time when he would make use of them. First of all he had to sneak out some documents, then make out a plan. He had to be careful.

Joe started the engine and drove home. Two blocks down the street, a white 504 Peugeot followed suit. There were two young men in the white 504. One was driving and the other, tall and heavy built, brought out his mobile phone and dialled KK Johnson's number.

*   *   *   *   *   *   *   *

She paused and stared at the bunch of keys on the door. Marina shook her head, her husband had been mysteriously furious in the morning and had forgotten to lock the door to his study. That was the first time such a thing was happening, she wondered what was bothering Joe. Her instinct told her that it was something to do with Joe's work and that she could find a clue in the study. It suddenly occurred to her that she had never entered her husband's study. She opened the door and found herself in a spacious room with a desk, three comfortable chairs, a small library and a few other furniture. The floor was neatly tiled, just like the rest of the house. It was like an office. There were papers strewn on the table.

Marina went behind the table, sat down and in no hurry, glanced through the papers. She was intruding but she didn't care. She had to find out the root of Joe's worries, she said to herself. But she also knew she was lying to herself, if she found out Joe's problem, there was nothing she could do to solve it, she knew it and she knew she was only trying to find out more about her husband's business.

Chioma was sick with worry. It was past 1.00 a.m. and not a sign of Pearl nor her bodyguard. Something was wrong. She could feel it. If only she had the slightest idea of where they were!

'This is quite unlike Pearl,' Chioma thought aloud 'something must be wrong, it is too early to call the police, and what would I even tell them.' She sighed in exasperation and switched off the television with undue force.

Pearl sat on the narrow iron bed, which was the only furniture in the tiny room where she was locked up. She stared blankly ahead of her. She had been sitting that way for hours upon hours, doing a lot of thinking. The question that roamed about her head was 'why?' Chioma was right, Pearl admitted to herself with a wry smile, but does she have to learn the lesson the hard way?

Ify and Linda had been acting, pretending. They were fake friends. Their only reason for being at De Plaza was to help whoever hired them, to kidnap her. They were real professionals. Linda pretending to be in love with Sam and taking him away, just to make their task easier, and Ify, inviting her out with what she thought was a genuine enthusiasm.

Ify's so called friends turned out to be two men. One of them, Pearl later knew as Ezeobi. Pearl's surprise came when they stopped the car in front of a shop and Ify got out on the pretext that she was going to pick something from the shop, the car sped off and Pearl, panic stricken, struggled in vain to get out from the car but the two men were too strong for her. They were armed with guns. Pearl had called after Ify, who obviously heard, but didn't even turn her head.

'Ify, you can't do this to me!' Pearl had wailed as the car sped off. 'Ify, I trusted you!'

There was something Pearl didn't understand. Why were they doing this? How did they know she was coming to Enugu? She heard the key turn and a man brought her some food. He tossed a crumpled piece of paper at her after he had kept the food, then he left, locking the door after him. Pearl opened the crumpled piece of paper and read the almost illegible writing:

'I can arrange something for you, it only requires N600, 000.00 and a little amount of cooperation from you.' Pearl read it over and over; she was suddenly filled up with hope. She smiled. It was her first smile since she was kidnapped. Her stomach rumbled for the umpteenth time and she was forced to look at the food beside her. She ravenously attacked the food. It was rice with stew on top.

After she had eaten, Pearl lay on her back on the narrow bed, which squeaked in protest. From the conversation in the car, Pearl gathered that one of the kidnappers, the one they called Ezeobi lived with his family somewhere in Enugu. They called the place Abakpa. It was certain someone hired them. Pearl had closed her eyes after she had struggled in vain, perhaps they thought she was asleep when they were discussing. She also learnt that their 'oga' or whatever they called their boss lived in Lagos and that Ezeobi will travel to Lagos tomorrow morning through Apex transport.

A light tap on the door. She heard it again and cautiously climbed off the bed. She went near the door.

'Who is that?' she asked in a barely audible voice. The key slowly turned and the door was quietly opened. It was the 'kind man.'

'What do you think, do you like my offer?'

'Of course I'll pay it if you will help me. Just get me out of this place.' They were talking in undertones.

'Come with me.'

Pearl hesitated, 'Now?'

The man nodded and she followed him through a dark narrow corridor. They went out into the cold night air.

'So easy!' Pearl exclaimed in surprise. 'I can't believe'

'Ssh! No time for talking.'

The place was not fenced, so they just crossed over. They passed two other houses then they went towards the third house by the left. He opened the door and signaled for Pearl to enter. She did.

'You stay here for the meantime.' He locked the door. Pearl leaned on the door, tears of disappointment rolled down her cheek. She sighed loudly and beat her clenched fists on the door in frustration. She had simply thought he would bring her back to the resort and they would then make arrangements as to how the money will be paid. She realized how silly it was for her to think that way. She should have run away when they were outside!

Pearl looked around her. There was a bed at the corner of the room. It was much bigger and looked more comfortable than the former one. There was a chair and a table. There was another door! She hurried to try the door but much to her chagrin, it was locked. She tried the window, it was open, but had iron bars across. Pearl studied the room. She noticed a wire that protruded from under the bed. She squatted on her knees and peered under the bed. What she saw excited her; she delved under the bed and brought out the telephone.

Chioma turned sleepily and grabbed the receiver. She suddenly sat up as she heard Pearl's desperate voice.

'Oh dear, where are you?'

Pearl rushed on and told her everything, every slight detail about what happened, not forgetting to mention Ezeobi. Pearl gave her a full description of Ezeobi and told her everything she gathered from their conversation in the car. Chioma carefully wrote down every detail.

'So you have no idea where you are now?'

'Not the slightest idea, but I know I'm still in Enugu. How do you get the money? I want to get out of this place!'

'I'll call your dad'

'Chioma…' Pearl stopped as she heard a key turn in the door. She was still holding the phone. The 'kind man' entered the room.

'I see you're a fast girl' he said, coming towards Pearl. His face was a mask. Pearl instinctively stepped back. The man's lips were smiling, but his gaze remained cold and hard. His eyes were like two black diamonds. 'I should have checked this room! Who were you trying to call or who did you call?'

'My friend. I was calling her to help me get the money, but then how do you get it?'

He eased down on the chair. He looked quite unruffled.

'Don't worry about the money right now; we have to escape from my colleagues. My boss won't hesitate to kill me if he finds out, but since

I'm not scared of death and I desperately need the money' he shrugged, 'then let's carry on with it.'

'Where do we start?' Pearl dropped the phone.

'One of my colleagues, Ezeobi is travelling in the morning he won't find out unless he checks on you which I doubt he would. Anyway, before then we'll be on our way out of Enugu.'

'Out of Enugu?' Pearl shook her head emphatically 'but…'

'Look, our lives are in danger. Ezeobi trusted me so much and left me in charge and I betrayed his trust, I know he won't hesitate to kill me.'

'So what are we going to do now?' Pearl asked. She was getting impatient.

'I didn't plan this. I just started it on impulse, but now I think I shouldn't have started this, you were safe out there, our boss ordered us not to kill you or expose you to violence. I am taking risks...' he hesitated, and then got up resolutely. 'Let's set off. Time is against us.'

He took her by the arm and propelled her towards the door, to the waiting car.

'God! A flat tyre!' he exclaimed furiously as he kicked the back tyre with undue force that it ended up hurting his leg. 'Wait in the car while I fix the spare tyre, and don't try anything funny' he added in a menacing tone.

*   *   *   *   *   *   *   *

Marina turned for the umpteenth time. Each time she turned she noticed that her husband was still awake. She had a clue of what was bothering her husband. Her worst fears were confirmed in those documents she read earlier in the day. Her husband was involved in organized crime. Her husband was a Master. Marina shivered involuntarily.

'Why didn't you tell me earlier?' she asked Joe as she settled more comfortably on her side.

'Tell you what?'

'You're a Master Joe.' She said it ever so quietly. Joe remained silent for a long time. When he came back earlier in the day and had found out he forgot his keys on the door, he had wondered whether Marina went inside his study.

'What have you got to say about it?'

'A lot.'

Joe turned to face Marina. He would tell her everything, in detail.

8

Ezeobi stopped the car in front of the unfenced building. He entered, calling out 'Taiwo.' His voice echoed in the silent building. He walked through the narrow corridor, stopped in front of the room where they had locked Pearl up. The door was ajar. He stood still for a second, trying to figure out what might have gone wrong. Their prisoner was gone. He raced further up the corridor and opened the door to another room where Taiwo was supposed to stay and guard the prisoner.

'What is trying to go on?' he muttered to himself as he went down the corridor again. As he passed the room where Pearl was supposed to stay, his eyes fell on a crumpled paper on the floor. He picked it up and read the note. It was Taiwo's handwriting. Ezeobi swore under his breath.

He sat in his car staring straight ahead, trying to decide his next line of action. Something ahead of him caught his attention. He peered in the darkness, he didn't have to debate whether it was Taiwo's car. Without being told, he started the engine, he would find out what Taiwo was up to.

Taiwo noticed he was being followed and increased speed, but nobody could beat Ezeobi who was very experienced, he was right behind them. Taiwo was a good driver too and he made things difficult for Ezeobi. Ezeobi brought out his pistol and aimed at Taiwo's rear tyres.

They were forced to stop. Taiwo got out first and faced Ezeobi who had also got out from his own car. There was a tense silence as the two men stared defiantly at each other. Taiwo spoke first.

'Exactly what you've always wanted, huh? What brings you out from your house by 3.00 a.m.?'

'I received a call from Lagos. Oga wants you in Lagos by 7.30 a.m. So that means taking a flight.'

'Don't tell me that was what brought you out in the middle of the night,' Taiwo replied, eyeing him questioningly.

'Actually, I should have come very early in the morning to inform you, but he sent me somewhere and I should be there by 5.30 a.m.,' he shrugged. 'Unfortunately for you, my premonition got the better of me and I decided to come immediately,' he answered levelly. He was moving towards Taiwo.

'How could you?' Ezeobi barked out through clenched teeth, he was holding Taiwo by the collar.

A fight ensured between the two men, Pearl got out of the car and tried to run away. She ran blindly, trying not to make any noise and attract attention to herself, but unfortunately for her, she stumbled and involuntarily let out a cry. Before she could get up, she heard a loud noise, which echoed, accompanied by a sharp pain burning savagely on her shoulder. She opened her mouth to say something but the pain was too much for her. Her head was bursting with pains and everywhere was coming towards her. She was feeling dizzy. She crashed unconsciously on the ground.

There was silence for a long, long time as the two men stood facing each other, a defiant expression on both faces, eyes blazing with fury. Taiwo spoke furiously through clenched teeth.

'You've killed her! You know what that means? Do you know the amount I would have gotten for her ransom? Anyway,' he added menacingly, 'we have both lost, Oga will not hesitate to snap the life out of you... with his bare hands.'

Ezeobi let out a hysterical laugh, 'I'll kill you first, and I'll make sure of that!'

Like a mad man, Taiwo rushed wildly at Ezeobi, intending to knock down the pistol. Before he could do it, Ezeobi pulled the trigger and Taiwo staggered back, slumped on the ground, eyes glazed and only the whites showing, blood spurting out from his stomach. The dead body was grotesquely spread out in the street.

* * * * * * * *

Enugu was again filled with the usual early morning rush. Civil servants hurrying to get to work on time, parents hurrying to get their children to school on time, noise of hawkers and newspaper vendors as they went about their businesses. All these, broke the serenity of the previous night.

However, on street 21, things were different. A large crowd gathered near the two bodies sprawled on the ground, about thirty feet apart. Some of the spectators were trying to reckon what exactly might have happened. It was quite clear they were shot. Some of the passers-by just stopped to take a look, then went about their businesses, shrugging, muttering a lot of things about the incident.

Amidst the noise and confusion, someone shouted, 'Hey! Get an ambulance, the girl is alive!'

Pearl moaned faintly as she struggled to gain consciousness. She could hear voices but they seemed to come from afar. Her head was pounding like mad, but the pain on her shoulder was more excruciating. All of a sudden the voices became louder, like a roar. The noise was bursting her head.

'Give her breathing space!' someone was shouting as she gently slipped back to unconsciousness.

Some minutes later, an ambulance arrived, followed by the police. On seeing the police, the spectators fled, all except the neighbour who had called the ambulance.

Pearl was taken to the nearest hospital. As for the other body, it was taken to the state general morgue for identification.

On the second trial, Chioma got Mr. Mbakwe on the line. It was 6.00 a.m., she discovered as she idly glanced at the table clock.

'Hello,' came the businesslike voice at the other end.

'Good morning, may I speak with Mr. Mbakwe.'

'Can I help you?'

'I'm Chioma, Pearl's friend, we have a problem down here...' She paused as she frantically thought how to relay the message.

'Is Pearl alright?'

'Pearl has been kidnapped' she blurted out. There was silence at the other end.

'And her bodyguard?'

'I don't know.'

'I'll be right there. De Plaza resort. Room number?' Joe dropped the receiver and paced about the room.

'What are they trying to do to me?' he whispered to himself as he absently scratched his head. He dialled the phone.

'Hello, is that Musa?' Book a flight for me, yes the next available one to Enugu. I'm going alone. I don't need a bodyguard. Em... don't tell anybody I travelled, understood?' He packed some papers in his briefcase, and went inside their bedroom through the connecting door, which he locked after him. Marina was sitting up in bed when he got there.

'Pearl has been kidnapped.'

Marina turned sharply, shaking her head frantically, 'tell me you're joking, Joe.'

'I'm not. Chioma just called and informed me. I'll rush down to Enugu and see what I can do,' he sighed.

'That's all you get by being a Master,' Marina said sarcastically as she got up. 'I think we have three prime suspects right now.'

Joe cast her a questioning glance.

'The Mafia, the Vikings, or even your fellow

Masters.'

Joe nodded, he adored his wife and wished things were different.

Marina continued, pacing slowly, 'If you rush down to Enugu, who'll plant the explosives, remember you have only a day, and besides, they'll question your absence at the office.'

Joe sighed deeply, sitting down at the edge of the bed.

'Help me make a plan, Marina.'

Two policemen were guarding Pearl. They knew that if the killers found out she was still alive, they would do anything in their power to stop her from testifying, if she would. The only visitor allowed to visit Pearl was Mrs. Adisa, the lady that called the ambulance, a very kind woman in her late forties.

'How is she getting along?' Mrs. Adisa asked the doctor.

'She'll certainly make it, though she lost a very large amount of blood from the bullet wounds, then she had concussion, she hit her head on a stone. She's responding quite well to treatment, anyway, and the shock is subsiding.'

'That is impressive. Em... has she said anything? I mean....' She shrugged, 'you certainly know what I mean.'

'Sorry madam, but whatever she says goes to police report and not to you,' the doctor smiled politely. 'If you'll excuse me, I have some patients to see.'

'Has she opened her eyes at all?' she asked and the doctor stopped in his tracks and turned.

'She opened her eyes, but slept off immediately,' then out of curiosity, 'do you know her?'

Mrs. Adisa smiled, 'No, but I'll like to see her recover. She must have gone through hell. Well,' she added 'thanks a lot doc., I'll just sit beside her for a while.'

'No madam.' It was one of the policemen by the door. 'Sergeant Bola said nobody should stay alone with her until she gets very conscious.'

'Of course you can stay with me,' she told the policeman.

Mrs. Adisa sat on the stool beside the hospital bed where Pearl lay. She looked down at the pale girl on the white hospital sheets and silently prayed she would survive. The girl on the bed reminded her of Nelly, her daughter. She had a car accident and she didn't survive. Nelly was about the same age as this girl lying on the bed. Pearl's shoulder was covered by a bandage moist with drainage from a concealed bullet wound. There were scratches on the side of her face.

Mrs. Adisa had always been a softhearted person and she was glad her two sons got that trait. It helped a lot when she was widowed four years ago. Her two sons were her only consolation. Thinking about her sons, she looked down at the girl on the hospital bed and thought how nice it would be to have another Nelly in the house. She would make a good wife for Stanley. Strange thoughts!

Puffing out smoke from his mouth, Chief KK Johnson stared out of the window in his study. He stubbed out the cigarette and turned to face Larry, one of his agents.

'Find out exactly what he is up to. I know he has no relations here in Lagos, what business has he got with an old woman in Lawal Street. I want you to watch him closely. Very closely, and be careful, Larry.'

'Yes sir.'

'Larry!' Larry turned as he reached the door. 'You have to work fast. I'll kill you if he outsmarts you.' Larry knew it was a serious threat.

Joe parked his grey Pathfinder on the parking lot. He paused for a while before opening the door. He had to appear bright as if nothing had happened, as if nothing would happen.

Joe walked into his office, carrying his briefcase. His secretary was already there, arranging the table. She looked up and smiled, her boss was happy.

'Good morning sir.'

'Isn't it a wonderful day? It's my birthday,' Joe said as he dropped his briefcase on the desk.

'Happy birthday sir.'

'Thank you. Come on,' he said, propelling her to the door, 'we've got to celebrate, I have some few things in my car. Would you mind bringing them in? You can tell the receptionist to help you.' He handed her his car keys.

There were seven cartons in the car. The cartons were all sealed but two were cartons of biscuits while the rest was wine. The secretary and two other employees packed the cartons in one side of Joe's office. Joe nodded his approval as he mentally counted the cartons. They all had biscuits and wine inside except one. When they had all gone out of the office, he locked the door and brought out the carton that had explosives. He opened his desk drawer and emptied them there, then stuffed the empty carton inside the waste paper basket. He brought out the instructions together with the office layout and studied them.

On the office plan, he studied the points marked 'x'. He wasn't surprised when he saw he had to plant one in his own office. The rest were at different points, two on each floor, then one at the toilet of the topmost floor. He would plant them, but getting the documents except those in his office, was impossible. He wouldn't implicate himself further.

Chioma hurriedly opened the door at the first knock. She was surprised to see Chidi standing there. The lady at the reception had told her Mr. Mbakwe, and she was expecting Pearl's dad. Chidi had changed incredibly and since they left secondary school she had never set her eyes on him.

'Chidi come in, I didn't recognize you instantly, and it's been such a long time, besides I was expecting to see your dad.'

'He sent me,' he said sitting down on the sofa. 'Sit down and tell me all you know about the incident,' he brought out a small tape recorder and pressed.

Chioma sat tensely on the sofa.

'I'm waiting,' she heard him say. She cleared her throat.

'I'll start from the beginning.'

'Then do!' he said impatiently as he took out a cigarette from his pocked and lighted.

There was silence when Chioma finished narrating the story.

'Why didn't you call the police?'

'It was too early to do so, I waited for Pearl

until around one o'clock, then I went to bed.'

'You went to bed....'

'Wait a minute Chidi, I know this is quite a blow for you but I can't bear it either, if anything happens to Pearl. Don't blame me....'

'OK!' Chidi said with an impatient wave of hand. 'Let's go straight to the central police station to see the much they can do for us, then I'll send some men to investigate further.'

Inspector Oladipo listened attentively as the two people facing him narrated their story. He was a stout man with a heavy paunch that made him appear shorter than he really was. He was a good listener, never interrupted. He opened the topmost drawer in his desk and brought out a file, which he opened and wrote down the report, eyes squinting as he read it over, and then handed it to Chidi.

'Cross check it and see whether I missed anything, then both of you should sign below.'

Inspector Oladipo said to Chioma, 'You said you wrote down all the information Pearl overheard?'

'Yes,' she gave him the paper.

'OK. I see,' he said when he finished reading it. 'We'll see what we can do, I'm sorry I have to keep your report. You were smart enough to have written down every single detail, you'll really make a good detective,' he added with a smile.

Chioma signed the report in the file and handed it back to the inspector.

'Do you have any of her recent photographs?' he asked Chidi as he got up and went over to a shelf in the corner of the office to keep the file.

Chidi fetched his wallet and brought out Pearl's photograph. 'I always carry it with me,' he said. 'It was taken a month ago.'

The inspector took the photograph and studied.

'I want you to make this case as discreet as ever. No publication what so ever.'

'We'll try our best. May I have your address and phone number? I'll call you as soon as I come up with something.' They gave the resort's address and phone number then stood up to go.

'You'll hear from me,' the inspector told them as they shook hands.

When they had gone, inspector Oladipo sat on his chair and studied the photograph once again. Just then, a police officer came in.

'Report from Uwani and Abakaliki stations,' he said, keeping the files on the desk and went away.

Inspector Oladipo leaned forward in his chair and glanced through the papers. No serious case, just the usual cases of theft and fights. He picked up the second file and brought out the first report.

99

He squinted his eyes as he read, brows drawn together in concentration. The case was rare, and a serious one too.

Case No.1: Uwani Station
Date: 23rd October 1994
Time: 06:30 a.m.
Place: Street 21, Uwani, Enugu.

Two bodies discovered. They were shot by unknown people. The man is dead and his body is at the State General Morgue and yet to be identified.

The girl is alive. She was rushed to St. Peter's hospital to receive treatment. She is still unconscious and has not yet made any statement. Two policemen are there to guard her until she regains consciousness. Minor investigations are being made by the CID. A white 504 Peugeot car was found there. There were bullet holes on the tyre. According to records, the car was stolen two years ago.

'The main investigation depends on the statement she would make. No publication yet.'

'Sounds interesting,' Inspector Oladipo said to himself as he absently flipped through the second and third pages then came back again on the first page. This case excited him and he wanted to know more about the case. He let his stumpy fingers dial the phone. He was calling Uwani Station.

9

'This is Inspector Oladipo. Is Sergeant Bola there?' Some seconds later, Sergeant Bola was on the line.

'I just got your reports. Referring to case no.1, has the girl regained consciousness?'

'No, I haven't heard from them. I was just about to go there when you called,' he paused, 'can you guess what really happened, this case is unusual don't you think so? I bet they didn't know the girl was still alive.'

'I just hope she's safe, they would try and get to her.'

'I sent two men there.'

Oladipo shrugged, 'Anyway, I'm coming with you to see her at the hospital, just wait for me, I'll join you in a few minutes time.'

He stared incredibly at the pale girl on the hospital bed.

'I can't believe this,' he whispered audibly to

himself.

'Believe what?' Sergeant Bola asked, looking curiously at inspector Oladipo.

'Her name is Pearl, the missing girl.' Sergeant Bola cast him a question glance.

'Wait, I'll explain later, I have to contact her brother.' Bola shook his head in confusion as he watched the stumpy form march lithely out of the room.

Yes, she could hear voices, she tried to open her eyes but they have placed lead on both eyes. She closed them again and opened them, they were a bit lighter. She squinted her eyes, the light was bright. It was as though a screen of smoke was put before her. It was clearing slowly. She could make out something turning. It was a fan.

She turned sideways and saw a girl in uniform. A nurse? What was a nurse doing in her room for goodness sake? She looked around the room. God! Police?

'Where am I?' She asked in a barely audible voice. She suddenly made to sit up, but dropped back again on the pillow. Her shoulders were so heavy as if a load had been placed there. Her head also ached. The pain made her wince and she looked again at the faces in the room.

They were all smiling nicely to her and she was so confused. All of a sudden, something in her head seemed to explode as she heard the sound of a gun over and over again. She cried out loud, 'No! Don't kill me!'

The nurse was at her side and she calmed her down with a soothing voice. 'It's over, it's over, they can't touch you again, whoever it was.'

The nurse's soothing voice seemed to reassure her that everything was really alright, but something told her it was just beginning. Propping her up on the pillow, the nurse said, 'I'll get water for you, then maybe some light food then I'll call the doctor to check you.' She hurried out and one of the policemen came forward.

'I'm Sergeant Bola, I can see you are feeling quite stronger. I hope you can remember all that happened.' Pearl nodded with difficulty.

'In that case, we'll work together, when you are much stronger, you'll talk to us.' He smiled and told her how they were found, not forgetting to mention Mrs. Adisa.

'Thank God there are at least a few good people in Nigeria to make up for the bad ones.' She said in response to Mrs Adisa's help.

'I know you are blaming me for what happened to Pearl, I only wanted her to share this holidays with me, I had a slight premonition that something wrong was going to happen, but my dad urged me to invite Pearl to keep me company.' Chioma shrugged, picking at her food. They were having lunch at the restaurant in the resort premises.

'Your dad knows Pearl?' Chidi asked.

'Yes.' She smiled 'I talk a lot about my friends.'

'What is your dad's name?' Chidi asked casually.

'He is Chief Obi.'

Chidi tensed. 'SK Obi?'

'Yes. You know him?'

'No... em... yes, I've heard about him in the papers,' he lied. Chidi dropped his spoon. His appetite has disappeared. His worst fear has been confirmed. SK Obi, the Vikings are responsible for this. But why kidnap Pearl?

'Are you alright?'

Chioma's voice jolted him back to the present. He fetched a stick of Dunhill and lighted.

'I just remembered something urgent I have to do,' Chidi said. He wiped his mouth with a napkin and leaned back on his chair, nursing his cigarette.

'You are close to your dad aren't you?' Chioma shot him a questioning glance.

'Not all children talk to their dad about their friends,' Chioma smiled. 'He's quite fond of me, maybe because I'm his only daughter. He'll do anything for me, sometimes it scares me.'

'Your dad must be a wonderful person. I would like to meet him' Chidi said.

'He'll call by two o'clock and he will certainly come over the moment I tell him Pearl has been kidnapped. He'll feel responsible for what happened to Pearl....'

'Don't,' Chidi said authoritatively.

Chioma looked up.

'Don't ever tell him about what happened to Pearl. Just tell him Pearl is alright, enjoying herself.'

'But why?'

'I've said it, and if you dare mention a word about it to your dad, Chioma,' he added menacingly 'you'll regret it.'

They crossed the wide entrance of the resort and were about to pass the reception area when the lady at the reception stopped them in their tracks.

'Miss, you had a visitor' she said to Chioma. The lady brought out a piece of paper and handed it to Chioma.

'It is from Inspector Oladipo, he said he has great news for us.' Chidi took the note and read.

'I can't go with you to the station, I have to wait for my dad's call. When you're back I'll hear the latest development.'

Chidi gave her a cold look. He didn't say a word and he went out. Out in the street, Chidi hailed down a cab.

'Central Police Station,' he told the driver as

he settled in the back seat. He brought out his mobile phone. He was calling his father, Joe.

'Dad....'

'Have you found her?'

'Not really. The police are helping us....'

'The police? Why the hell did you report to those bastards....'

'Dad cool down, they even have a positive news for us and that's where I'm going. I'm inside a taxi.'

'Well, you have to turn back. I'm coming to Enugu and we'll go together to the station OK?' It sounded like a question but Chidi knew better. It was an order. He told the driver to turn back to the resort.

'Dad, I found out who was responsible for Pearl's kidnap.'

'Who?'

'Chioma's dad.'

'Who is Chioma's dad?'

'Dad you know I'm inside a taxi. No privacy.'

'Come on, lets be careless for once,' Joe said impatiently.

'Chioma Obi's dad.' Chidi stressed on the 'Obi.'

'You mean SK Obi?'

'Exactly.'

'That bastard!'

'But it is not necessary for you to go. Chidi can handle everything, first give him instructions,' Marina protested when Joe came home later and told her about Chidi's phone call. Joe was in the study and Marina was in the bedroom. The connecting door between Joe's study and the bedroom was ajar. Since Marina knew everything, there was no use in locking the door except when he was going out. Marina was tidying up the bedroom.

'I have to go and make sure that the police do not investigate further on the case. I'll arrange private investigations.'

'What about our plan?'

Joe let out a tense smile. 'The birthday stuff went on fine. The explosives are in my desk drawer. I'll go to the office in the night and plant them.' Joe yawned as he came out to the bedroom. 'I'm hungry, what's for lunch?'

'Garri and vegetable soup.'

'Mmm my favourite'

'Everything is your favourite when you're hungry,' Marina said, folding the last dress on the bed.

'Marina,' she turned to look at Joe.

'Chidi found out that SK Obi was behind Pearl's kidnap.'

Marina hesitated and sat at the edge of the bed.

'I'm not really surprised. Maybe he wants to use Pearl to swap for the documents when you get them. He wouldn't want you to cheat them.'

Two hours later, Joe and Chidi came inside the inspector's office. Inspector Oladipo was busy behind his desk, but when he saw them, he quickly got up, grinning from ear to ear.

'Great news,' he said. 'Your Pearl has been found.' He looked at Joe.

'This is my father,' Chidi said to the Inspector. Inspector Oladipo shook hands with Joe.

'Have a seat, Mr. Mbakwe. Chidi, you too.'

'You said you've found Pearl?' Chidi said unbelievably. 'Within twenty-four hours? That's great.'

'Where's she?' Joe asked. They were still standing.

'Please have seats.' They obliged. Oladipo brought out Pearl's file and brought out the report on the incident at street 21, Uwani. He thrust the report on Joe's hand.

'Read this,' he said.

'What has it got to do with Pearl?' Joe queried when he finished reading the report. Chidi took the report and read.

'Everything.' Oladipo said. Joe cast him a questioning look.

'The girl is Pearl. I went to the hospital after reading the report. I recognized the girl from the photograph Chidi gave me.'

'Let me see the photo,' Joe said. Oladipo brought the photograph and Joe put it in his pocket.

'You can't have it,' Oladipo said, but Joe ignored him.

'Is she alright?' Chidi asked.

'Yes. Two policemen are guarding her at the moment, so she's safe from the killers. When she regains consciousness, she will make her statement. We'll investigate further....'

'No,' Joe protested. 'I want you to close all investigations. No further investigations....'

Oladipo stared incredibly at him. 'But why? If we don't find the killer, other citizens might fall victims. No,' he shook his head, 'this is no ordinary case to close,' he snapped his fingers, 'just like that.'

'I have a very genuine reason why I want the investigations to stop. This case is very complicated. It is something I have to settle by myself. Here,' Joe brought out his chequebook from his inner pocket and tore out a leaf. 'How much?'

'Sorry sir, but I can't and I won't accept anything from you. Further investigations on this case must proceed and you can't do anything to stop it.'

Chidi watched the two parties in fascination. Joe studied the inspector for some moments. He would try once more and if he did not yield, he would use threats.

'Ten thousand naira and no further investigations,' Joe said, Oladipo shook his head. Joe smiled.

'I'm not adding a dime, instead I'll start subtracting,' Joe said, Oladipo shook his head.

'I told you...' he began, but Joe cut him off.

'You're taking ten thousand my friend!' Joe didn't raise his voice.

Inspector Oladipo sighed and paced the length of the room, absently scratching his baldhead. 'How do I know that it is not a bounced cheque?'

'If it is a bounced cheque, continue with the investigations, but,' he added as he got up and quietly approached him. 'If you take this money and still continue with the investigations, I'll tear you apart.' He paused. 'Have you ever heard of Masters of the Underworld?' Joe let out a short laugh as he brought out a pen and filled the cheque.

'Now take us to Pearl,' Joe said after he had given the cheque to Oladipo who was staring at Joe with mouth agape.

'Wait at the outer office, I'll join you in a moment.'

When he was alone in the office, Oladipo brought out an old photograph from his desk drawer. The middle-aged man in the photograph looked so much like the Inspector. The man in the photograph was his father, a top custom official. Inspector Oladipo was very close to his father, there wasn't any secret between them. When he was in secondary school his father died.

That was when the presidential election was about to take place. One of the presidential aspirants, Chief Yashidi was rumoured to be a Master of the Underworld as well as a drug baron. Inspector Oladipo's father, Henry had told him that Yashidi was actually both. He dealt on cocaine.

Before Henry was promoted, he couldn't do anything about it. He guessed his boss was being blackmailed by Yashidi, Yashidi knew something that would completely ruin the boss and he used him. Through his boss, Yashidi trafficked his drugs.

Eventually his boss retired and Henry was promoted, that was during the presidential election, Yashidi needed more money for his campaign and everything. He wanted to export some kilos of cocaine but Henry wouldn't take the five hundred thousand naira bribe that was being offered to him. They used threats but Henry wouldn't oblige. Henry even threatened to report him to authorities and the next day, Henry had an accident on his way to the wharf. Inspector Oladipo sighed loudly, he knew the Masters of the Underworld, Chief Yashidi, in particular, was responsible for his father's death. He knew it was no accident.

The urge to revenge was so overwhelming, the urge to expose all the Masters to the Federal Bureau of Investigations.

He was in a position to do it. He was a police officer.

'You killed my father, you damned idiot!' Oladipo said aloud with bitterness to relieve some of the anger in him.

10

KK Johnson faced his only son. They were at the balcony facing the front of the house.

'Andrew, you're wasting.'

'What do you mean I'm wasting dad?'

'I didn't send you abroad to waste, look at you,' he regarded his tall lanky son for a while, 'As my only son, I have tried to give you the best things in life, money, love, you've had your own way ever since you were a kid, and look at what I got in return, a spoilt child who has immersed himself in hard drugs.'

'Dad I need the money,' Andrew said unrepentantly.

'And the worst thing,' KK continued, 'is that you didn't come home to see me or to stay with me, but to ask for more money. You're working Andrew and despite that, the allowance you get from me is thrice your salary in that bank....'

'I'm out of job dad, they said I was involved in fraud.'

'Andy, you are going back to America and your flight ticket is all I'll pay for. I won't give you a dime. Go and make yourself useful and stop hard drugs.'

'I'm not begging you, dad,' Andrew stood up, went to the bar and poured a drink for himself. He sipped the fiery liquid tentatively as he came towards his dad who was sitting on a sofa, lighting a cigarette at the moment. He towered above him. 'You are despicable, dad; first of all, you killed my mum. I was still a kid when the accident happened, an accident indeed! But I can recall the conversation and the arguments you had with her the whole week before she died. Secondly, you didn't really revive Masters of the Underworld, the Vikings are the real Masters. I have a solid evidence, and many more, dad... many more.'

KK Johnson got up and slapped his son, his fingers made a light pink print on Andrews face. The impact of the slap made Andrew's drink to spill all over his hands.

'You can even kill me just like you killed mum.'

KK slapped him again and again, but Andrew continued, his voice higher, 'Mum found out you were a Master, she found out many ugly things about you and she threatened to expose you, she....'

'Shut up, son!' The shrill of his mobile phone interrupted KK Johnson. He picked it up from the side table.

'Larry what's new?

... but I'm sure today is not his birthday....

... Enugu? Wonder what the bastard is up to. Have you checked 12 Lawal? OK.'

KK Johnson sighed deeply. Joe Mbakwe was asking for it. The man must have something up his sleeves and if that was so, he must be eliminated.

'Well, what do you say to me?' Andrew's voice jolted him back to the very present. His son was blackmailing him just as he had and is blackmailing a great number of top officials in the government.

'Do you know you're a Master, Andrew, that when I die you....'

'Come off it dad! What do you say to me?'

'You'll get your money tomorrow.'

The door was slightly open and Joe gently pushed it open, ignoring a uniformed policeman near the door. Behind him were Inspector Oladipo and Chidi. Joe paused at the door to look at his daughter, who was lying on the hospital bed. Pearl was sleeping.

They came inside the room; another police officer was there. Oladipo was saying something to him.

'Dad! Chidi!' Pearl said in a weak voice as she opened her eyes.

'Poor dear! What have they done to you?' At that instance, Joe took three capable strides that brought him to her bedside. He took her hand, being careful not to hurt her on her wounded shoulder.

'I want to go home,' Pearl said

'Yes. We'll get you out from this place. I'll talk to the doctor. Now, rest.'

Some minutes later, Joe was in the doctor's office, trying to persuade the doctor to discharge his daughter but Dr. Eze wouldn't hear of it.

'Your daughter has not yet recovered from shock, and moreover she lost some blood. She is still very weak and there are series of tests that she has to go through. We want to make sure there are no internal damages.'

'I want her transferred to Lagos, to another hospital there, this is very important, doc.'

He finally succeeded, and thirty minutes later, Pearl was discharged from St. Peter's hospital. Inspector Oladipo drove them to the resort where they collected Pearl's items. Chidi also helped Pearl to dress up.

When they got to De Plaza, Chioma was not in the room, they collected the spare key from the reception. Oladipo later drove them to the airport.

Precisely 5.20 p.m., the airport taxi finally

came to a halt on the driveway of the Mbakwe's residence. Marina spotted them from the window, came out and headed towards them.

'Mum' Pearl said faintly as Marina and Chidi helped her out of the taxi, careful not to hurt her wounded shoulder. Pearl's head was covered with bandages, so was her shoulder.

'Pearl don't worry, you'll soon recover. You're home and quite safe.' Marina said as they mounted the short steps that led to the front door.

'Did anyone call me?'

'KK Johnson called,' Marina said. 'He wanted to see you, I told him you had migraine and I had to give you some aspirin, together with sleeping pills, that you couldn't come to the phone.'

'That was very thoughtful of you, dear,' he turned to Chidi. 'Send Musa to get Dr. Okoro.'

When they entered the house, Joe's mobile phone rang.

'Yeah?....

... tonight, eleven O'clock....

... I'll be careful, listen this would be the first and the last task I'll be doing for you guys, don't ever use the cassette stuff to threaten me....'

There was an irritating laugh at the other end.

'It is not the last task, Joe. The final task, which I know you'll benefit from, at least three million dollars, is to get the documents for the Vikings.'

'It doesn't really concern you if I get the documents for them.'

'It does, Joe,' the hoarse voice at the other end continued, 'we are aware that Vikings are the real Masters, we have a score to settle with them, but' he stressed on the 'but', 'I want them to get those documents. Meanwhile, eleven o'clock tonight....' And the line went dead.

Inspector Oladipo dialled the phone in his office. This was his fifth trial. The line had been busy. Luckily for him, it went through, Lagos lines were always busy, Mondays through Fridays.

'Hello, Inspector Oladipo on the line....'

'Hey boy! Thought you've forgotten me.'

'Paul, you're sick! Why haven't you called me? So how did you find your transfer? I know you're missing Enugu'

'We are sweating here boy! Got a lot of bad guys down here.'

'That is what I want to discuss with you Paul. Do you know an organization called Masters of the Underworld?'

'What about them?'

'I want them extinct.'

'That's impossible boy! Many have tried and failed and you know the funny thing? They don't live to tell their tales, so be careful.'

'That's too discouraging, I thought you would

help me.'

'I'll help if that is what you want, but I won't stick in my neck so deep boy! I love my life.'

'Paul if you hear more about this organization, you would want to stick your neck so deep that you won't mind getting stuck. They killed my dad.'

There was a long silence at the other end. When Paul spoke again, his tone was serious.

'Is that why you want to nail them? You want revenge. You have to reason dear, you have a wife and two kids, you can't just decide to throw your life away....'

'I am not throwing my life away, it's not just revenge, those bastards are taking more than enough. One of them came to my office this afternoon, Mr. Mbakwe was his name, he lives there at Lagos, maybe we could start with him; Paul they use their influence, their money to intimidate others.'

'You mean they intimidated you...' There was a chuckle at the other end.

'Come off it Paul...' There was a knock at his door and two men came in.

'I'll call you again and please do get serious. I have clients right now.'

He dropped the phone and faced the two men.
'Have seats....'

It was 8.00 p.m. when Joe started the engine of the black 504 Peugeot. He was going to see KK Johnson. He wasn't going to let KK get suspicious.

A servant opened the front door and asked him to wait at the sitting room. KK Johnson was in his study and would be there shortly. Precisely twenty minutes later, KK Johnson came into the sitting room.

'Good evening sir.' Joe greeted him as he sat down on the sofa opposite him. KK merely nodded.

'It is quite a pity you had a migraine on your birthday,' KK said in his usual slow manner, eyes never leaving Joe's face. He didn't miss the hint of discomfort that flashed on Joe's face like lighting.

'How was your trip to Enugu?'

'Sir, there was no trip to Enugu.' KK stopped him with upraised hands.

'Anyway,' KK said. 'Ever since you signed that contract nineteen years ago, I have watched your every move and I'll say I am impressed. You never tried to double-cross the Masters and so far, you have carried out the assignment well but you and I have been blind about one thing. Those Vikings are a very cunning set of people. Have you ever asked yourself why everything is now at a standstill? Why they seemed all of a sudden to lose interest in what they have been planning for nineteen years?'

'Sir, everything is not at a standstill.'

'Then why have you kept everything to yourself? You should be reporting to me on daily basis and in details, everything. That is an offence, Joe.'

'I'm sorry sir.'

'Why do you say everything is not at a standstill?'

Joe leaned closer. 'Somehow, they found out I was a spy, working for the Masters and I got a phone call, the caller threatened the Masters, he said he would destroy KK and Co together with all the Masters. He said…'

'When did you get the call?' KK interrupted.

'Today sir.'

KK nodded and Joe continued 'He said he had a story that would be useful to me and I could make some money with the information. I dropped the phone on him.'

'Tell me,' KK said, 'have you ever had a meeting with a Viking, I mean face to face or even phone calls?'

KK Johnson's shrewd eyes didn't miss the instant shuffle of feet. He knew Joe was nervous. The question made him uncomfortable.

'Just this phone call,' Joe said looking at KK Johnson squarely on the face. KK Johnson nodded, eyes never leaving Joe's face.

'I called your house, did your wife inform you?'
'Yes sir.'

'I called to inform you we have an ad hoc meeting tomorrow, KK and Co. I made a decision this morning. We are going into drugs. We are liaising with the Masters in Togo. The meeting is just to inform them and also to share out responsibilities.' Joe was silent. He hated this idea of going into drug business but there was nothing he could do about it.

Once KK said something, that's that. Nobody can change anything about it. Joe was sure of one thing, if the meeting would hold it would never be in KK and Co because tonight, he would bring about a ravage....

'What sort of drug are you talking about?' Joe asked.

'Amphetamine.'

The two men talked about the drug. KK Johnson was very optimistic on the success of their drug venture. Why amphetamine? Joe had asked during their conversation but KK ignored the question and started talking about something else. Finally, Joe looked at his wristwatch, it was 9.45 p.m. He still had an hour and fifteen minutes.

'I think I had better go home and get a good rest.'

'Yes you look tired, one of my bodyguards will take you home,' KK said, Joe didn't argue.

'That would be fine,' Joe said as he got up.

'I wonder why you decided to celebrate your birthday two months in advance. Anyway,' he said still sitting down, 'I have a birthday present for you, an advice, don't ever lie to me.' KK Johnson got up and went out of the room. He went upstairs leaving Joe standing at the center of the sitting room.

Just then a man came in and said he was asked to take Joe home, he would follow him to his house and then turn back.

10.47 p.m. Joe Mbakwe headed for KK and Co. He was inside a taxi, quite oblivious of the brown Toyota that trailed them. The taxi stopped at a safe distance from the gates and Joe Mbakwe went towards the building. The two men in the brown Toyota, not far from the taxi, watched as Joe talked to the guards at the gate. They opened the gate and Joe went inside the building. There was another guard at the main entrance of the building.

'Good evening sir,' he greeted as he opened the door for Joe. Joe nodded. 'You forgot something sir?'

'A file. The birthday stuff disorganized me a lot.'

'Happy birthday sir,' the lean guard said with a toothy smile. Joe nodded and faked a smile in return.

'Anyone else in the building?' Joe asked a bit too casually. The guard shook his head 'Chief Okoh just left his office some minutes ago.'

'I see,' Joe said, entering the building. All the lights were on, for security reasons.

Joe went inside his office and locked the door after him. He unlocked his desk drawer and brought out the seven explosives. He brought out the building plan together with the instructions. The instruction says, insert the cap, connect the two wires and twenty minutes, the bomb will blast. Joe packed the explosives in a briefcase in his office. He would start from the topmost floor of the seven- storey building. He glanced at the office plan again, and then carrying the briefcase, he went upstairs. He would plant one on each floor including the one he would plant in his own office.

It wasn't as difficult as Joe thought it would be, and within ten minutes he had planted five explosives. He was planting the sixth one at the corner leading to Mr. Alan Giwa's office when he heard footsteps. He froze at the corner, the footsteps stopped in front of Joe's office at the other end, after some seconds, Joe heard it fade away towards the entrance of the building. He quickly connected the wires and left the explosive there. He checked his watch, he had spent fourteen minutes planting the explosives, six more minutes and the topmost floor would blow. He hurried to his office. He gasped when he almost collided with a guard.

'Sorry to frighten you sir, I was wondering...'Joe ignored him and went inside his office still carrying the briefcase. Inside his office he quickly inserted the blasting cap and connected the two wires. He opened a safe in his office and brought out all important documents which he dumped into the empty briefcase. He quickly came out, locking the door after him.

Out in the street, the taxi was still there, Joe heaved a sigh of relief as he entered the taxi. The driver sped off. Joe Mbakwe didn't want to be there to watch the company crumble like a pack of cards.

The brown Toyota was still there; they didn't bother to trail the taxi back. They were waiting, watching. Three minutes later, the topmost floor of KK and Co blew with so much noise. They could see the guards running for their lives. The rest of the building blew up at intervals. However, they did not wait for the whole building to blow as they sped off into the cold night air. Within a few minutes the grandeur of KK and Co, import and export was down in depredation, leaving a crumbly residue.

11

The very first thing Joe Mbakwe did after planting the explosive was to go home and call SK Obi on the phone. It was precisely 11.40 p.m. when Joe got home and silently opened the front door. Marina was there, and she got up as soon as Joe came in.

'I hope it was a success,' she said and Joe nodded. 'You have to contact SK Obi as soon as possible; KK Johnson would definitely suspect you. He has never really trusted you.'

'What has SK Obi got to do with this for goodness sake!' Joe slumped down on the sofa and unbuttoned his shirt.

'You need their protection. They would do anything to protect you because they are desperate to get hold of the documents, and of course they won't get it if anything happens to you.'

'You think I need protection?'

'You should know better.'

Joe Mbakwe got his mobile phone and called SK Obi's private line. 'This is Joe,' he said as SK picked the phone. 'Sorry if I woke you up.'

'Yeah, you already did wake me up. Listen, I'm very busy right now, if you have any positive thing to discuss, I think you should come to my house.'

'But it is not safe for me!'

'I'll send a car right away.'

'Alright,' Joe said as he sighed deeply.

The two guards waited at the huge gates, still panting, while the security man at the gate called Chief KK Johnson on the phone.

'Sir, two guards from KK and Co are here to see you. Something terrible has just happened'

'Send them in,' KK said in a curt voice as he wore his housecoat over his short and rushed downstairs. He met them in the hall.

'Sir, the company has just blown to pieces.' KK Johnson slapped him over and over again.

'I just hope you're not drunk,' KK said in a drawling tone.

'No sir,' the second guard continued, stepping back at safe distance. 'I didn't know how it happened, but all of a sudden the whole building exploded, starting from the topmost floor. It happened just as Mr. Mbakwe went out of the building....'

'Mr. Joe Mbakwe?'

'Yes sir, he came to collect some papers'

'Was there anybody with him?'

'No sir, but he came just as Chief Okoh went out of the building....'

'You can go. I'll call you when I need you.'

He left them and went inside his study and dialled his phone.

'Larry? I think you have to plant those drugs in his house.'

'Why not wipe him off and continue with your business. He's taking more than required boss.'

'Not yet Larry. I want him to suffer in prison. There are some things I have to find out before wiping him off.'

'Your wish is my command boss'

'I want it done soonest Larry, and be careful. Check out Chief Okoh too. He too might have something up his sleeves. My company has been blasted to pieces'

'I'm sorry sir, and you think Mr. Mbakwe has something to do with it sir?'

'A lot. He is our prime suspect.'

Forty-seven minutes later Joe was sitting face to face with Chief SK Obi. They were in SK Obi's sitting room. They were alone. Joe spoke first, trying hard to control his anger.

'I'll do the job for you if you have a reasonable

price. I hate bargaining so you fix a decent price and stick to it.'

'Alright. You said you'll think of it for three million dollars. I'll add another two.'

'That is settled. The money will be paid into my private account in the Swiss bank. I want it done next week.'

'I will pay in 2.5 million and after I get the file, I'll pay in the rest.'

'But there's no guarantee that I'll get the remaining money if I hand over the documents.'

'OK. I'll pay in all, but you're dead if you try anything funny.'

'That's OK. It's a deal. What about protection?'

'You'll get twenty-four hours protection, we'll even protect the whole family.'

'Even the one you tried to kidnap and swap for the documents?' Joe said in a bitter voice.

'If you were in my shoes you would have done the same. I didn't hear from you and I was so desperate.' There was a long silence.

'You'll get the first set of documents as soon as you pay in the money.'

'Your protection starts tomorrow morning. I'll send some boys for you.'

It was 6.45 a.m. when the bedside telephone rang. Joe's eyelids were still heavy with sleep. He turned and placed a pillow on his head. Marina picked up the receiver.

'For you,' she told Joe and gave him the receiver.

'There has been an explosion at KK and Co,' KK Johnson's voice rasped out. 'I've sent men to investigate on the cause. I'll contact others. There'll be a meeting in my house around 2.00 p.m. Stay at home till then. I might need you.' He dropped the phone without waiting for Joe's reply.

'Just told me about the explosion,' Joe said to Marina. 'Said I have to stay at home till 2.00 p.m., that he might need me.' Joe turned and leaned on one elbow, facing Marina.

'I wonder how I'm going to spend this long morning. Any suggestion?'

'Yeah. Just stay in bed,' Marina said and Joe grinned

'You mean the two of us! Wonderful.'

'No alone,' Marina said jokingly.

'You can't be serious dear!'

Joe Mbakwe was taking a shower, whistling loudly in the bathroom, oblivious of what was going on in his sitting room.

'You can't search this house,' Pearl said to the two policemen in uniform. 'This is the wrong place. We don't deal on drugs.'

The second policeman, a man in his early thirties spoke. 'Where is your father?' Pearl was silent and he continued. 'This man behind me,' he said gesturing towards Larry who was standing with an amused expression on his face, 'has confessed that Mr. Joe Mbakwe has been his client, buying hard drugs from him for quite sometime....' Before he could finish, Pearl rushed upstairs to call her dad.

Joe rushed downstairs with only a towelling robe, followed by Marina and Pearl.

'What is happening officers?'

'You are suspected of being a drug dealer. We want to search the house.'

'You can go ahead' Joe said confidently 'but I can assure you that you are in the wrong place.'

They all followed the officers as they searched the whole house, leaving no stone unturned.

'What about the ceiling? That's where most of them keep their dopes.' Larry suggested a little too casually.

'Yeah, you've dealt with it long enough to know,' the younger policeman said, examining the ceiling.

'They look untouched,' said the second officer, 'but I think one has been touched. It looks a little out of place.' They were in the store upstairs. He fetched a stool, climbed on top and pushed open the ceiling. He groped inside the dark until he brought out two bags of whitish substance. They all gaped and then accusing eyes turned on Joe who was dumbfounded.

The officer opened them, took a pinch from each of them and gave it to Larry to examine.

'Cocaine and amphetamine.' Larry said after testing them.

'Mr. Mbakwe, you are going with us to the station. You are under arrest.'

'I've been set up! No! This is a set up. I've been framed!' Joe wailed. Larry's face was lit up with a complacent smile. He had done it! Pearl looked at Larry. She didn't trust him.

'Chidi, Dad has been arrested,' Pearl screamed into the receiver. 'They found drugs in our house, they were planted Chidi, dad has never dealt on drugs. They framed dad....'

'Calm down, Pearl. Is mum there?'

'No. She went with them. I'm alone.'

'When did this happen?'

'Just now. I wonder who the hell framed dad, Chidi.'

'Pearl I'm coming right now.'

Pearl dropped the receiver and dialled. She had another call to make.

'Hello,' KK Johnson's slow drawl filled Pearl's ears.

'Uncle KK, dad has just been arrested,' she

wailed into the receiver.

'Don't play your pranks on me kiddo.'

'But it's true, uncle. Two policemen and another man, came, searched the house, found drugs and arrested daddy. They've locked up my dad. Uncle please do something about it.'

'Sure kiddo. I'll go to the station right now and see what I can do. Don't worry, uncle is there to help.' KK Johnson dropped the receiver and tried not to laugh aloud at the irony of it all.

Chidi came in some minutes later and after listening to Pearl's side of the story, tried to think straight. He knew it could be the Masters, the Vikings or the Mafia. But the Vikings wouldn't because he can't get the documents for them, locked up behind bars, and it couldn't be the Mafia either. So that leaves us with the Masters.

They heard the sound of a car in the driveway and rushed out to the front door to meet Marina.

'Did uncle KK come to the station?' Pearl asked as Marina came closer towards them. They both turned to Pearl, waiting for an explanation. 'I called him to let him know and he said he would be there to see what he can do.'

'Pearl, if you have nothing more to do than to call people announcing that your dad has been locked up, I think you had better go up to your room or find something better to do,' Marina said, walking past them as she went inside the house.

Pearl stared at Marina's back, a confused expression on her face.

'She is tensed up. Her husband has just been arrested' Chidi told Pearl as he followed Marina upstairs.

'Chidi, call SK Obi and inform him. Follow me to the study, I'll give you his number and I'll feed you with the latest development. I have a premonition that KK Johnson framed my husband.'

'What makes you think so?'

Pearl eavesdropped in rapt awe at the conversation going on upstairs. She wanted to hear more.

They called SK Obi and informed him of Joe's arrest. He promised to take immediate action. He was actually suspicious that KK Johnson had something to do with it. Maybe he found out about Joe's deal with Vikings and he decided to keep him away for a while. SK Obi knew he didn't take drugs. His men had left no stone unturned when they were asked to find out everything about Joe.

'Any problem sir?' SK Obi turned to face a small-framed man in his early forties, a fellow Viking and a close associate of his.

'Joe Mbakwe has been framed. They've planted drugs in his house and he was locked up this morning. His wife just called. Never knew he discussed everything with his wife.'

'And our deal with him?'

'I'll still pay in the money. I'll get him out of there. You'll go there right now and talk to our men over there.'

'Yes sir'

Pearl leaned on the doorpost to his daddy's study. Chidi and Marina looked up in astonishment.

'What makes you think uncle KK planted drugs to frame dad?' Pearl asked with a defiant expression on her face. She looked Marina squarely on the face and she stared back.

'You've been eavesdropping, Pearl.'

'I overheard. Why do you leave me out, mum? You'll tell Chidi the latest developments but why am I not included?'

'Jealous?' Chidi chipped in 'you'll soon know everything and I'm telling you, you won't like it a bit.' He turned to Marina, 'Mum, it is high time she knew what has been going on since 1972. She's still uncle KK's little kid and I think Pearl could help us a great deal. Don't you think so?'

Marina nodded. 'Pearl, close the door, sit down and just listen. Hold yourself, listen, reason dear, don't blame anybody, don't hate anybody after this revelation.'

Chidi sat behind Joe's desk, legs crossed on top of the desk. He was silent, fiddling with a pen.

Marina sat on top of the desk, absently dangling her legs. She was facing Pearl.

'Have you ever heard of the Masters of the Underworld?'

'I wonder what it has got to do with our talk' Pearl replied.

'Just answer the question' Chidi said.

'Who hasn't heard of those unscrupulous people who terrorized the rich men of Nigeria before the civil war' she paused, 'I've heard a lot about them, it was some sort of anarchic society, smooth operators, professional blackmailers. One thing I liked was that they didn't involve themselves in any fetish practice. I wonder why they collapsed during the civil war....'

'They still exist, Pearl and they run our lives.'

'I don't understand.'

'Dad is a member' Chidi blurted out. There was a long, uncomfortable silence.

'Chidi why can't you stop your silly jokes for once in your life!'

'That is a fact, Pearl,' Marina returned calmly. 'Sit down, let me tell you the story of Joe's life and how he got involved with them.'

Pearl sat down and listened with rapt attention to the incredible revelation. They told her everything they knew, even the vows and the conditions.

12

The airport taxi wormed its way through the hectic traffic on Lagos roads. Inspector Oladipo sat at the back seat, he was excited. Two days ago he had received a call from Paul. Mr. Mbakwe was arrested for drugs. Cocaine and amphetamine. He was still locked up and Paul thought this case would lead them to the Masters. Mr. Mbakwe would be tortured. If he talks, then that would be a good lead, Oladipo thought as he relaxed on the back seat.

'I'll get those bastards,' he thought as he lit a stick of St. Moritz and exhaled a thick smoke.

At the central police station, Lagos, the taxi screeched to a halt and Inspector Oladipo came out, paid the taxi driver and mounted the steps with undue virility.

'Hey boy! You're here already.' Paul said getting up from his desk as Oladipo entered his office.

'Yeah, two days is enough for me to clear the

desk. Two days of anxiety. Now, I would like to see our man.'

'He says he wants a lawyer. Really insisting he was framed, but I don't think so. The whole case is self evident.'

'I'd like to talk to him,' Oladipo said.

Pearl sat at the back seat of her father's ash coloured Santana. Their chauffeur was taking her to KK Johnson's residence. The incredible revelation had really shocked her. It all sounded like a bad dream, but she had to face reality. In a few months' time she would be twenty and she is supposed to take over, to be a Master. Even with the blasted KK and Co, which was just a mere front for the notorious organization, KK would still go ahead with the organization.

Pearl was so determined to act as a self-employed espionage, to find out everything she could about the Masters and their plans, steal out the documents and destroy the organization before three months, when she would be twenty years. That was Pearl's vaulting ambition and she would risk it. She would help her dad. She would never be a Master and her dad would never be sacrificed.

Initially, she had almost hated her dad for keeping it a secret from them, for allowing himself to be maneuvered so easily, for letting himself to be trapped... but she put herself in her dad's position and tried to think what she would have done if she were in her dad's shoes, and she pitied her dad. She realized that her dad must have gone through a lot. Her dad had been risking his life, trying to dissolve the Masters without implicating himself or his family. Even to the extent of planting explosives at KK and Co, working in collaboration with Vikings.... This realization made Pearl love her dad more and she felt a deep hatred for KK Johnson, for the Masters....

The security men opened the massive gates as the driver blared the horn for the second time. They stopped at the driveway and Pearl took a deep breath, came out and mounted the familiar steps that led to the front door to KK Johnson's house.

She eventually found KK at the balcony. He was relaxing on an easy chair, with legs stretched in front on a low stool. He beamed as he saw Pearl.

'Hello dear!' he said in his usual slow drawl. 'Sit down and tell me where you've been hiding for the past few weeks.' Pearl forced a bright smile and hoped it looked as real as it used to be.

'Uncle, is it really up to two weeks!' She exclaimed as she went to the bar to fix a sherry for herself.

'Kiddo, I'm really sorry about your dad. I wish I could help but' shrugged, 'it really has been a tough time for me, with my company down in depredation....'

Pearl's face was expressionless.

'Yeah, I know you would have helped if you could, I'm sorry about your company. What was the cause of the fire?' she asked innocently, sitting down adjacently to KK.

'It was an explosive. Investigations are still being made.'

'Billions of naira must have gone down with the building... and lots of important papers too!' Pearl sounded genuinely sympathetic.

'Anyway, I'm happy I kept the most important documents at least. Let's forget about this whole thing, what about a game of chess?'

Pearl grimaced.

'Am I boring you?' KK asked.

'Very untypical of you to say that!' Pearl exclaimed with mock horror. 'Since I was a kid, you've been playing cards and chess with me and I don't think I'll ever get bored staying with you. Not everybody would have the patience to teach a child how to play chess or cards.' She added with her disarming smile 'Uncle, you are my second daddy.' She looked him straight in the eye.

KK Johnson smiled in an almost shy manner. Pearl knew KK genuinely had a soft spot for her and she would make the most use of it. Just then the phone in the balcony rang and KK picked it.

They brought Joe Mbakwe to a small room with a table and three straight chairs. Inspector Oladipo looked at the same man who had walked into his office roughly a month ago, threatening and giving orders. He now looked at Joe's chin, rough with three days' beard, his hunched shoulders, and wondered if he was the same man.

'Remember me?' he asked Joe who remained silent. He was sitting at the head of the table and the two policemen sat on either side of the table. A small recorder was placed at the centre of the table. Oladipo continued, 'since you insist you were framed, you could perhaps talk to us, to enable us investigate and nail the criminal, you can't achieve anything if you stay locked up in jail. Talk to me, Mr. Mbakwe, or rather Joe. The Masters, do they have anything to do with this?'

Joe looked up sharply. 'I know you are a Master,' Oladipo continued in a mellow voice 'you told me yourself, Joe and you'll tell me more... if you don't want to remain in jail.'

Inspector Paul spoke, 'Maybe you want to say it the hard way, when you will be tortured to talk about the Masters. They are into drug business, aren't they? Aren't they?'

'Calm down Paul' Oladipo said. Paul had slightly raised his voice.

Paul continued, 'Don't think they would get you out of here, I won't take bribes from anybody, I don't get shaken by threats, and you had better talk before we nail the Masters... if you want immunity.'

Joe's body was sleek with sweat. He knew he would tell them all, starting from the very beginning. The immunity was very important to him.

Pearl couldn't exactly discern what KK Johnson was discussing on the phone. It had something to do with what they were expecting, maybe goods from abroad.

'... OK. Send the boys immediately. I'll call you in thirty minutes time, let me just confirm.' KK dropped the receiver and excused himself saying he had an urgent business in his study and would be back shortly.

Pearl had never been inside KK's study. She had never really had an opportunity to walk in there, and she was so curious to know what was there. She wondered if the important documents were in his study. The shrill of KK's mobile phone, which he had left on the stool, interrupted her train of thoughts.

'He is busy right now.' Pearl spoke into the

phone, 'but I'll call him since it is urgent. Just hold on for some minutes.'

A smile tugged at the corner of Pearl's mouth. This was a golden opportunity for her to enter KK's study. She ran down the corridor with the phone in her hands as she opened the door one by one. On her third attempt, she found the door to the study, she opened it without knocking and Pearl's hands flew to her mouth, her eyes wide with astonishment. KK Johnson turned sharply, closed his safe and covered it with a big painting but Pearl's keen eyes didn't fail to register a small red knob on the door to the safe. There were several other knobs with numbers written underneath. Pearl's eyes returned to look at KK Johnson who stared back with expressionless face.

'Uncle KK, I'm really sorry!' She exclaimed wide-eyed, looking as innocent as ever.

'I didn't know you had such bad manners, kiddo,' he said. 'Anyway, what brought you here in the first place?'

'I didn't mean to intrude. Someone was on the phone, he said it was an urgent business.' She handed the phone to KK 'I think I had better go home,' she said.

'I'm not angry at you kiddo, but if you really want to go...' he shrugged, 'before I forget, take those invitation cards on my desk. My 67th birthday is next week and I want you all to come....'

Back in the corridor, Pearl almost leapt with joy, she knew there were important documents in the safe. At least, that was a good start.

The two inspectors listened to the incredible story as Joe spoke, leaving out nothing. When he had finished there was a long silence, except the tick of the wall clock above their heads. Paul looked up and realized they had been there for hours.

'So you're supposed to get the documents for the Vikings?' Oladipo asked, still deep in thought. Joe nodded.

'Could it be that KK Johnson found out about your deal with the Vikings and decided to put you away for sometime?'

'Could be.' Joe said curtly, 'but he could easily have killed me.'

'He could have his own reasons,' Paul said, absently fiddling with his pen.

'And the Masters are supposed to start the amphetamine business?' Paul asked and Joe nodded.

'What do you think?' Paul asked Oladipo when they were alone in Paul's office.

'I think the story is genuine. Let's try him, Paul.

Let's give him a temporary freedom on the condition that he would get the documents and hand it over to us, inform us about the latest developments in their amphetamine business. We would make two fake copies of the documents and he would hand a fake copy to the Vikings. How does it sound?'

'He needs protection. KK Johnson might try something funny' Paul said.

'The Vikings would protect him. Joe has to be alive for him to get the documents for them, and moreover the police would also give him twenty-four hours surveillance.'

'Do you think it would work? I don't really trust this Joe guy. He might try something real cunning.'

'We'll risk it, Paul.'

'Mum, I'm sure there are very important papers in that safe,' Pearl said, pacing the length of their sitting room. 'If you see the way he shut it immediately and replaced the painting on the wall.'

'But there's no way we can get the papers without being caught,' Marina said.

'There is.' Chidi said, SK Obi should know someone, professional that can deal with any type of safe, most of them have alarms.'

'The birthday would be an opportunity to get it. Everyone would be so busy, but the problem is getting the professional inside the house without being caught,' Marina sighed in exhaustion.

The phone rang and Chidi picked up the receiver.

'It was from the police station,' he told Marina after he had spoken and dropped back the receiver. 'Dad has been released. We are asked to come and pick him up.'

'Chidi let's go together. Mum should stay at home for a change,' Pearl said.

A few minutes after they had gone, there was a blare of horn at the gate and from the window, Marina could see KK Johnson's black Mercedes Benz car as it pulled up in the driveway. KK Johnson came out. There was one other man in the front seat with the driver. Marina instantly recognized the face in the front seat. He was the man that came with the police to arrest Joe. Seeing him with KK Johnson, Marina was convinced more than ever, that KK had something to do with Joe's arrest. The front door bell rang for the third time and Marina opened it.

'Marina how are you?' KK said as he stepped inside the sitting room.

'You're welcome. Have a seat.'

'Actually, just dropped in to know how you are

doing. I'm on my way to see Joe at the station. Wish I could get him out of there.'

'There is nothing anybody can do,' Marina said, averting her face.

'Anyway, there are some papers I would like to collect from Joe's study if you don't mind. Some of our goods are in the wharf and we can't clear it without those papers.' KK said, pacing about the room and pausing now and then, to admire some paintings on the wall.

Goose pimples covered Marina's body. KK was cunning.

'But you sent people to collect all his documents yesterday. Haven't you gotten them?'

KK Johnson raised a quizzical brow 'Not me.'

'They were two men and they said you sent them, they even showed me a note from you!' Marina wailed, forcing false tears to streak down her face. She would do anything to preserve the little document Joe has got. 'I just hope I haven't given them to the wrong people!'

KK Johnson swore under his breath, trying to control his fury. 'How could you?' KK rasped through clenched teeth.

'Joe even told me before he went to jail, that some people were supposed to come here and collect all the papers, that I should let them. I even thought they were the same people you sent....'

'Dammit!' he swore and pushed Marina aside

as he went out of the house. 'I will really see him in jail' he said. He stressed on the 'see'.

Marina heaved a sigh of relief as she heard the car speed off.

'Never knew I was a born actress' she murmured to herself as she slumped down on the nearest sofa, closed her eyes and prayed that this should soon be over.

When KK Johnson reached the police station, Joe had gone, but Inspector Paul just told him that nobody was allowed to see Joe. KK Johnson tried to bribe him, even threatening him, but he didn't succeed. He was even more furious when he left the station.

Marina picked her mobile phone and called SK Obi. She didn't trust the house phone anymore; they might be bugged.

'Hello, this is Marina Mbakwe.'

'Hello!' SK Obi's loud voice boomed into her ears. 'I was just about to call you. We couldn't succeed in getting your husband out; the officer in charge wouldn't take money from us. Not even a dime. And he didn't get pissed off by threats.'

'He has just been temporarily released.'

SK Obi heaved a sigh of relief and Marina continued 'He is not safe at all. KK Johnson won't hesitate to kill him and I'm so scared.'

'Don't worry about security. Our men are reliable, well trained. They are watching your house right now and I was informed KK Johnson just came there, right?'

'Yes. He wanted some of Joe's documents. Said he couldn't clear his goods at the wharf without those papers.'

SK Obi laughed hysterically 'The idiot! He didn't get it or did he?'

'No.'

'He was only bluffing. We have men at the wharf. There are goods at the wharf, but not legal stuff, drugs. Joe Mbakwe has nothing to do with it. He just wanted to clear Joe's papers as a Master before wiping him off. He didn't want any paper that would implicate him. How does it sound?'

'I think that's right.'

'Just keep calm. I'll send more men. We need Joe alive as much as you do. We'll try our best.'

13

It was KK Johnson's sixty seventh birthday and he was having a dinner party in his residence.

'Joe I think you should stay behind. It is safer for you.'

'I'll stay behind, but I think my blood pressure will sky rocket by the time you come back,' Joe said, sitting up in bed.

'We are quite secured with men from the Vikings and the police. The man that will open the safe looks reliable, but the problem is getting caught.'

'Please, be careful dear. As for opening the safe, SK Obi got a real professional....'

There was a tap at the bedroom door and Pearl let herself in. She was looking great in her body hugging black dress that flowed down her ankles, and a short jacket with a golden coloured design. She had a matching sandal with thin golden straps and a clutch bag.

'Hmm! You are looking great,' Marina

exclaimed. She was putting on her shoes. 'Joe, help me with the necklace while I put the finishing touches to my make up.'

'Not as ravishing as you look, mum.' Marina was dressed in a flowered chiffon dinner gown that was just above her knees. Her hair was done high up and her make-up was just perfect.

'You look eighteen dear,' Joe said to Marina after he had fastened the necklace around her neck, then to Pearl 'Is Chidi ready?'

'Yeah, he's downstairs waiting for us.'

They stood on the front door steps and the driver brought the black Limousine on seeing them. He was not their usual chauffeur. He was the man who would open the safe. Also in the front with him was a bodyguard. The threesome entered the car and Joe waved as the car rolled off, raising a cloud of dust.

A few blocks down the street, a grey 504 Peugeot with three men inside, followed them. Behind them was a brown jeep. Policemen in mufti. They didn't trail them, they watched Joe's house. Joe was their object of surveillance.

Adjacent to Joe's house, three Vikings also kept watch of the house, quite oblivious of the police.

Many guests had arrived by the time they reached there. Most of them were outside, standing in small groups. Marina looked at her watch. It was 7.30 p.m. They were thirty minutes late; she liked it that way.

KK Johnson spotted them just as they came out of the car. He excused himself from a man he was talking with, and came towards them in his usual capable strides.

'Hello!' he beamed at them. 'Hello kiddo!' he called out to Pearl 'Come on and meet the other guests.' He gestured to them, and then noticed the two men at the front seat. 'Who are those?' he asked casually.

'Our chauffeur and guard...' Marina replied and was interrupted by Kate Adele who was looking sweet in her black dinner dress.

'Where have you been hiding, Marina!' she said giving her a casual slap in the back. 'Sorry about what happened to Joe....'

The party was in full swing when Pearl eventually got a signal from Marina. She excused herself from the couple she was talking with and joined her mum.

'You'll take the man to KK's study right now. KK is busy discussing with his guests, I don't think anyone would be upstairs. Chidi is keeping watch and you'll get a signal whenever he smells danger.' Marina talked in a hushed tone.

'Where's the man?' Pearl asked.

'Just go. He's right behind you. Walk casually.'

Pearl swallowed hard and nervously rubbed

her sweaty palms on her dress. With head held high, she casually entered the house and headed upstairs.

'That is a good girl' Marina muttered to herself.

'He is home alone.' Larry said to KK Johnson. They stood away from the other guests. KK nodded, a wicked smile tugged in his lips.

'Wipe him off and clear any paper you see in his house. Take two men with you.' He ordered and walked briskly away. He joined a group and started chatting heartily.

There was no one upstairs. Pearl glanced behind her, the man was right there. She pointed at the door to the study. The man squatted down in front of the door, studied the keyhole, then extracted a small object from his trouser pocket. He used it to open the door without much fuss.

By then, Pearl was as nervous as hell and her sweaty palms, which she rubbed on her dress from time to time, showed her nervousness. She kept on looking around her. She could hear the noise of the guests as they chatted merrily downstairs.

They entered the study and quietly closed the door behind them. She pointed at the big painting on the wall.

'The safe is right behind that painting,' she

said. The man just nodded and extracted some tiny instruments from the breast pocket of his suit. He cut a small wire running across to the bottom of the painting.

'The alarm,' he said. He then brought down the painting and went to work, pressing some buttons, loosening some knots and all....

Some minutes later, Pearl froze as she heard footsteps coming towards the study. The man suddenly brought out a small pistol from his jacket and stealthily went behind the door, drawing Pearl close. Pearl shook with fright as the footsteps stopped in front of the door. Just then she heard Marina's voice. She was talking with KK... then the footsteps went back and suddenly everywhere was quiet again, except for the dim voices and laughter of guests downstairs. Pearl heaved a deep sigh of relief.

'Have you opened it?' She asked when she eventually found her voice.

'I think so,' the man said as he loosened one last knot and pressed a red button. The safe opened as he turned a knob. There were four files in the safe. Pearl stuffed some papers into her bag which she had brought last minute instead of the clutch. She brought out the three remaining files wondering how to take it downstairs without being noticed.

'I wonder how I'll carry these without being

caught,' Pearl said frantically.

'You stay here, I'll go and organize a power failure,' and off he went, leaving Pearl and her pang of nerves. At the door he paused and on second thought threw his pistol to Pearl. 'For protection,' he said and closed the door.

Joe Mbakwe was awakened by the chaos outside. He had fallen asleep on the couch in front of the television. He put off the TV and went to the window to look. He had given orders to the security man at the gate not to open the gate for anybody. From the light on the gatepost, he could see his security men arguing with two men. One of them looked familiar. The security wouldn't let them inside the house and they said they had an urgent message. All of a sudden, everywhere was quiet. The two security men fell drowsily down and one of the men threw out something like a syringe. Joe was suddenly alert; they had come for him.

He ran upstairs and fetched his pistol from his desk drawer, and called SK Obi on the mobile. 'Your men should close in. They are here, they've come to wipe me off!'

After that he called the police 'Inspector, send your men before it's too late.'

'We are in the neighbourhood, we know what is happening,' came the reply in the phone. 'Stay in your study, put off the light and don't make a sound.'

It seemed an eternity when Pearl eventually heard footsteps coming towards the study. She gathered the files, ready to go whenever there was a blackout. A key turned in the door and Pearl's eyes widened. Her jaw dropped as she came face to face with KK Johnson. No more uncle KK, but the KK Johnson, leader of the Masters of the Underworld, the notorious KK that had blackmailed a number of prestigious people in the country, getting whatever he wanted. His face was as stern as hell and his eyes emitted a fiery coldness that Pearl never knew existed.

'I should have known that!' he said; his eyes still boring into Pearl's wide eyes. 'My innocent kiddo! With my documents and a gun to kill me. Your dad sent you huh? He must be one hell of a coward to send you. Now, give me that gun dear.'

Pearl moved back as KK came forward.

'Stay right there! I'll shoot.... I mean it.' Tears streaked down Pearl's face and she was overwhelmed with pent up anger.

'You can't Pearl. It will haunt you forever, dear....' Just then there was power failure and Pearl, still clutching the files and her pistol, crouched down and made for the door. KK

Johnson extracted a gun from his breast pocket and shot blindly. Pearl followed suit and shot blindly, then there was silence after a while, followed by a crash as KK fell face down on his desk.

The gunshots alerted everybody and the guests dispersed in confusion. Marina, Chidi, their bodyguard and the man that opened the safe ran upstairs; they were holding a mini flashlight.

Pearl threw the files to Chidi who caught them and ran downstairs through the back door. She gave the gun with hands that shook, to the man who had opened the safe.

KK Johnson's bodyguards came just as they ran out through the backdoor. Two bodyguards spotted them and pursued them, and amidst gunshots from the confused bodyguards, they made their way to the Limousine. They all tumbled inside the car and sped off. Chidi was clutching the files like a lifeline.

The bodyguards couldn't fire openly because of other guests but they were ready for a car chase, they were about to enter a car when one of them shouted at them to stop. He was talking from the window of KK's study. 'There's no use boys! Boss is dead.'

During the shooting that had ensued between Pearl and KK, Pearl had shot him unknowingly.

The lights came back. The bodyguards and

some Masters who were present during the commotion came in to see their Boss sprawled face down on his desk, a nasty bullet hole just on his forehead. Some papers strewn on the table were stained with blood. Nobody knew what really happened.

Pearl was still shaking, crying uncontrollably 'I'm a murderer' she kept saying.

'It was self defence, Pearl, it was self defence.'

The gate was wide open when they reached their house and Marina let out a horrified gasp when she saw two security men sprawled on the ground. They all ran out of the car, Chidi still clutching the documents, as they ran inside the house.

'Joe!' Marina called out. There was silence. Everything in the house was out of place.

They found Joe in his study with two policemen in uniform. They were going through some papers on the desk.

'Dad! I killed uncle KK!' Pearl wailed and Joe held her.

'Calm down dear, calm down.'

'Here are the damned papers.' Chidi threw them on the desk. Joe heaved a sigh of relief.

'It's over. Larry has been arrested together

with some Vikings that came to rescue me. KK sent them to kill me, the Vikings came to save me, and they all got arrested by the police. I'll hand over all the documents to the police, in our presence, they'll burn all documents that proved that I was a Master, then they'll fake the most important one, the one needed by the Vikings. I'll hand over the fake paper to SK Obi.'

'But SK should also be arrested.'

Inspector Paul spoke up. 'Joe, you will call SK Obi, do anything you can to make him come here, bring him to us and that would be the end.'

Joe picked up his mobile and dialled SK Obi.

'Hello, I need to talk to you. It is very urgent.'

'Why not come here Joe?'

'It is for your own good sir, I need you right now,' and Joe cut the line.

'Do you think that would make him come?' Pearl asked.

'Let's hope so.'

'The guards are still sprawled on the ground. You think SK would be a fool not to turn back and flee on the sight?' Marina said.

'Come on, let's tidy up.' Oladipo suggested.

After they had cleared the house, they sorted the documents. 'Burn these ones, Joe. They will implicate you,' Oladipo said, handing the papers to Joe.

Chidi brought out a lighter from his pocket and

lighted the papers. They all stood looking as the papers slowly caught flame, watching the papers turn to ashes. Burning up evidence.

As soon as they heard the sound of a horn at the gate, one of the bodyguards opened the gate and SK Obi emerged from the car with two of his bodyguards.

Joe came downstairs to the sitting room, opened the door and let SK Obi in. 'Don't you think your bodyguards should wait in the car?' Joe asked and SK just shrugged.

'It doesn't matter, does it?' he said and without waiting for an answer, sat down and continued. 'Why do you want to see me?'

'SK, the game is over. I just decided that I'd hand the documents to the police. There is no evidence that the Vikings are the real Masters.'

'You are a fool, Mr. Mbakwe. You've been the ball for almost twenty years now and who are the players... the Masters, the Vikings and the Mafia. The Masters have used you, the Mafia has used you and the Vikings would use you. Joe you are getting the papers for us and in three days time, I'll pay the rest of the money. That was our deal.'

'I don't want your damned money!' Joe blurted out.

'Then you won't have your damned protection!' SK Obi spat back. 'KK Johnson would kill you with his bare hands!'

Joe let out a tight laugh. 'KK Johnson is dead.'

'What is your game?' SK Obi asked, dimming his eyes in suspicion.

'My game is upstairs if you really want to know, you are invited,' Joe said as he stood up. He went towards the staircase and could feel six pair of eyes boring at his back.

SK Obi got up and went out to the front door; his two men close behind. Their car was not there. There was not a single car in sight.

'He is trying to trap us,' SK Obi said thoughtfully looking around him. 'Didn't know I could be a damned fool!' he exclaimed swearing silently.

'What about taking a taxi?' one of the guards suggested.

'I came here with my car, and I'm going back with the same car.' SK Obi brought out a firearm from his pocket. 'We are going upstairs. The silly idiot should learn not to play his silly pranks. Don't shoot unless absolutely necessary.'

They went upstairs and didn't find anybody.

'Joe?' he called. Silence. His anger was panting up. They were in a corridor with rooms on both sides.

'Looking for Joe?' They turned sharply to face a policeman in uniform. SK Obi couldn't conceal his surprise. This was the last thing he expected.

'Yeah, I'm a friend of his.'

Oladipo flashed a toothy smile. 'And probably going to shoot him,' he said eyeing the butt of

SK's gun that jutted out below his shirt. 'Don't try anything funny; there are a great number of us here, watching you at this moment. SK Obi, just surrender. Now you should all hand me your guns.'

SK Obi did the decent thing and kept his firearm on the floor and the two bodyguards followed suit. Oladipo whistled softly, another door opened and Inspector Paul came out with handcuffs. They have got them.

Just then, Joe emerged and sauntered casually towards SK Obi. He stopped a few feet away from him and the two men stood, scrutinizing each other with cold fury. Joe was holding the files.

'In your presence, SK Obi, I'll hand over these documents to the police. You can chew your five million dollars. I will have my freedom, peace and privacy of not being followed.' He gave the files to Oladipo.

'The game is not yet over, Joe. The rest of the Masters would get you even if the Vikings don't.' They took SK Obi away together with his men.

The next day, Joe received a call from Inspector Oladipo.

'I think you are still not safe, Joe. Nobody double crosses the Masters and gets away with it. You'll still have twenty-four hours police protection until your papers are ready. The whole Mbakwe family would be going on an exile to any country you like.'

'Who is sponsoring the trip?' Joe asked.

'The federal government.'

14

It was a bright Sunday. A beautiful day. Two months after Joe Mbakwe and his family left Nigeria for their exile to South Africa.

Leaving Nigeria was not easy for them especially for Chidi who was still in school and who had to leave his girlfriend, Jenny. He could remember the night before they left Nigeria. He was with Jenny at a small café. He didn't know how to tell her he was leaving Nigeria. Jenny would want to know more and he couldn't tell her lies.

Inspector Oladipo had seriously warned them not to tell even their closest friends about the trip, it would be too risky, too dangerous.

'Why wouldn't you share your problems with me, Chidi? Something has been troubling you for the past few months and every time you see me, you try to cover up but I can see through your mask. You are always restless which is very unlike you.'

'Jenny, I'll miss you,' Chidi said slowly, eyes never leaving Jennifer's face.

'Chidi are you alright? What the hell....'

'This is supposed to be a secret Jenny,' Chidi said leaning forward in his chair as he continued in a low voice 'we are leaving Nigeria tomorrow...' and he told her everything. He trusted Jenny.

'You seem miles away.' Chidi turned sharply to look at his dad who was searching the picnic basket that was beside him.

'I was thinking of Jenny, dad. Two damned months! I can't believe it's just two months since we left Nigeria. Seems like two years to me,' Chidi said.

Joe sat down on the beach sands beside Chidi and they both silently watched Marina and Pearl at the far side of the beach. They were picking shells.

'Nigeria would never be a safe place for us, dad. Even after ten years, the Masters and the Vikings would do everything in their power to revenge. They'll revenge.'

'That is if they still exist,' Joe said. But they both knew they were invincible. They were everywhere.

To Joe Mbakwe, his stay in South Africa was

like a whole new world, living his life like others, enjoying the privacy of not being followed although at times he got this creepy feeling that he was being followed. He kept looking over his shoulders, suspecting people. He was almost going paranoid. Shadows of the past kept creeping up on him. Shadows of those he had been ordered to frame, to eliminate, to blackmail....

'I hate to admit it son, but I'm a very weak man. See how many years it took me to extricate myself from the Master's web, and in the process tangling myself in the web of the Vikings and the Mafia.'

'You were protecting yourself dad, so you had to do it in a quite insidious manner... and you've succeeded unlike Sonny Adele and many others who had tried to betray the Masters,' Chidi replied.

'Mine was just pure luck. I survived the first gunshot from Vikings. I don't know why KK didn't just wipe me off. Why did he have to plant drugs in my house?.' Joe shook his head.

'KK Johnson was a weak man, he was not powerful as an individual, he was hiding under the facade of the Masters. He was not a powerful leader and was not so good at making decisions.'

Joe heaved a sigh, 'Call Marina and Pearl, let's get going I'm expecting Inspector Oladipo's call by three o'clock.'

*　　*　　*　　*　　*　　*　　*　　*

Mr Alan Giwa was a small-framed man in his early fifties. His sharp prominent eyes made him look like he was frightened of something. He had been a Master for twenty-six years and he had never attempted to betray the Masters. Not because he wouldn't like to, but because he had seen what happened to those that attempted.

He was the man in charge of Sonny Adele's murder. It had been carefully planned between him, Larry and KK Johnson. KK had sent Sonny on an official duty at Badagry and they parked a car along the express way with the bonnet open. Any passerby would think they had a problem with their car. Alan and Larry leaned on the car, information had reached across that Sonny should pass there between 11.00 a.m. and 12.00 p.m., in a black Daewoo Espero. They should flag down any Daewoo Espero that passed, but so far none had passed.

11.37 p.m. they flagged down Sonny Adele. Alan could still recall everything that happened. Sonny came down from his Daewoo with a surprised look.

'Alan what are you doing here? It's a pity, I can see your car has left you stranded.'

'Thank God you came sir,' Larry said as he went over to the bonnet and closed it. 'We are having engine problems, we are on our way to Badagry.'

'I'm also going to Badagry, we'll go together,' Sonny suggested.

'We can't leave the car here,' Alan said. 'Your driver would take care of our car, Larry would drive the Daewoo to Badagry.'

It was settled and the unsuspecting Sonny entered the front seat with Larry, Alan was in the back seat, behind Sonny and it wasn't very difficult for him to suffocate Sonny....

Alan never did any of these jobs because he enjoyed it or because he was paid to do it. He did them because there was no way out. He was in, and for the Masters, when you are in, you are in and the only way out was death. He was happy when he heard that KK and Co import and export has been bombed and he was even happier when he heard that KK Johnson has been shot dead.

The explosion at KK and Co import and export, and the death of KK Johnson brought about remarkable instability among the Masters. There was struggle for power and authority among members. There was bloodshed among some of the top officials. It was a cold war. They went ahead with the drug venture and Chief Okoh was in charge. Andrew Johnson had put him in charge.

Alan Giwa was in his chauffeur driven Santana, on his way to answer Chief Okoh's call.

3.55 p.m. Inspector Oladipo called Joe's rented apartment in Pretoria. He had news that would bring a wide smile on Joe's lips. Joe picked up the receiver. He knew who it was.

'Joe how are you?' Inspector Oladipo spoke and without waiting for answer, continued. 'Larry spoke to us. He was almost at the point of death when he spoke. The Masters are now full time drug barons, KK Johnson's son, Andrew, put Chief Okoh in charge. They deal on cocaine and amphetamine. They import the cocaine but can you believe that a well-known pharmaceutical company here in Nigeria supplies amphetamine to the Masters. The Masters export some of the amphetamine to other African countries. They have a warehouse right under our noses, at Victoria Island.'

'You guys have to round them up,' Joe said.

'We are determined to do it. I have the names of the entire top ranked Masters in Lagos and their addresses. We'll get them. I promise. How is South Africa?'

'We are trying to adapt. I got a job in an advertising company. I'll start next week. Chidi is still behaving like a bear with a sore head, it wasn't easy for him leaving school and most of all, his girlfriend, but Marina and Pearl are the ones enjoying South Africa.'

'Mmm, I see you're not enjoying it,' Oladipo said.

'I'm trying to. Sometimes I feel someone is following me, trying to blow my head into bits.'

'You are only imagining things; I hope you don't end up being paranoiac,' he laughed 'I'll call next week.'

Chief Okoh lived with his wife in a small one storey building in the outskirts of Victoria Island. His two sons were in Germany. He was a man that loved power. He loved being in control. To him, it wasn't a bad thing that KK Johnson was murdered since it would bring him to the top, but he had a problem. The information he received in the morning was troubling him, it was genuine, he knew, because it was from a man who was burning with the spirit of vengeance.

Chief Okoh lay on the couch in his sitting

room, he was in a pensive mood, and he was scheming. A servant came to tell him that Mr Alan Giwa wanted to see him.

'Send him in.'

'You're late,' he said as Alan came into the sitting room.

'Traffic hold up,' Alan said, sitting down.

'SK Obi sent a message to me. I think we have to work in collaboration with the Vikings.'

'I don't understand. SK is still in detention'

'Nevertheless, he still has his ways. Joe Mbakwe betrayed the Masters and the Vikings, he destroyed the Masters, his daughter killed KK Johnson, Joe bombed the company. I want you to find his whereabouts. The man is not fit to live, we still have to maintain our old age tradition, nobody betrays the Masters and gets away with it....'

'That would only implicate us more. Let's face facts, our boss is dead, all our documents in the hands of the federal government, the company gone, there is chaos among the Masters. All that is left for us is the drug business. I think we should just concentrate on that....'

Alan tried hard to convince Chief Okoh but he was so adamant.

'Find him, Alan and kill the bastard.'

'There's no way I can find him. He vanished with his family into the thin air.'

'I know a way, an elixir to our problem,' Chief

Okoh said, a wicked glint in his eyes.

Jennifer Okeke, ladened with packages of groceries and provisions, came out from Cindy Supermarket. She stood on the pavement by the roadside, dropped the packages near her feet, brought out a white handkerchief and wiped the perspiration on her forehead. It was a very hot afternoon and she silently prayed it wouldn't be long before she found a taxi.

She did not wait for long before a taxi stopped in front of her. There were two people at the back, a man and a girl. The front seat was vacant.

'Moremi hostel,' she told the driver who nodded as she gratefully settled in the front seat.

Three minutes later she felt a prick on her right arm and turned sharply. The man behind her was small framed, with eyes that made him look like he was frightened. The man threw out a syringe from the window. At that instance, Jennifer grasped what was really happening but before she could say something, she started feeling drowsy; her eyelids felt as if a load was placed on it, her head was heavy. She was really saying something but she wasn't in control, it was like her brain had gone numb.

The two at the backseat, together with the driver laughed at the girl's reaction to the drug and the jumble of words she was saying as she fell into a deep slumber.

Through a cloudy haze she could see a man sitting by the bedside. Her head was heavy and she was famished. She looked around her. She was in a bedroom with a dressing table in one corner, a wardrobe at the far side. It was homely and at the same time, strange. She turned again to look at the man sitting beside the bed. She sat up and cringed to the far end of the bed. She recognised the man. The man that sat behind her in the taxi. The man that drugged her.

'What do you want?' Jennifer asked.

'I just need some information. Where is Chidi Mbakwe?' The question caught her off guard; Alan could see it. He could also see the fear in her eyes mixed with a determined spirit. He knew it would be difficult to extract information from this girl.

'Who is Chidi Mbakwe?'

'Where is he?'

'I'm sorry you got the wrong person. I've never heard that name, and I want to go back to my hostel.'

Alan laughed out aloud. 'Get ready for a long stay, girl, you have to cooperate. You are not leaving here until I see Chidi face to face.'

'Then you have to keep me forever,' Jenny

said shaking her head. 'I don't know him and you are asking me where he is. I would never know, even if you kept me here for a century.'

'You are Jennifer Okeke, Chidi's girlfriend for several years, and if you don't know his whereabouts, nobody else would know. Look here babe, my advice is that you should give me the address before you would be subjected to torture. You will pray for death to come, but Jennifer, I promise you, you would kiss death but it wouldn't take you dear, I promise.'

When Alan left the room, a man brought food for her. Garri and vegetable soup. After Jennifer had eaten, the man handcuffed her without much difficulty. He gave her a resounding slap that caught her off guard, she fell on the floor and looked up at the tall man who was no match for her. She dared not fight back. She cringed backwards, waiting for his thick palms to descend on her again but it didn't.

The man sat on a chair. 'I don't know what to do with you.' he said, 'what form of torture do you want? Beating? Skinning alive? A little bit of electric shock? Oh! I know.... Rape.'

'No!' Jennifer screamed.

'Scream again and I'll gag you up!' the man threatened. 'You are quite pretty and I don't want to disfigure you. Now, tell me... where is Chidi Mbakwe?'

Alan Giwa spoke into his mobile phone, 'They are all in South Africa, I know exactly where to find him.' he said to Chief Okoh. There was silence at the other end.

'Alan, you are going there as soon as possible. Wipe out the traitor. Be careful,' Okoh ordered. He loved giving orders.

Everything was arranged and the next week, Alan was in the plane, on his way to South Africa. Jennifer was still locked up.

There was another man who loved power to the core. Power was an obsession to him. Whenever he was in control, that was when he felt alive. He was not a Master neither was he a Viking. He was a Mafian. Oscar Ahmed, the man that had been sent to destroy the Masters. He had done the first phase of his work, destroying the company, KK and Co. He had been in the brown Toyota that trailed Joe and he had watched, a wicked smile on his face as the building exploded and slowly crumbled. He was aware of the instability among the Masters after the death of their leader, KK Johnson. He was happy about that. He was also happy that SK Obi and some of his men were in jail. He was happy that the documents were handed over to the police. He didn't really know whether the Vikings were the real Masters, so he was happy that both organisations were going down the drain. Thanks to Joe Mbakwe.

However, Oscar Ahmed felt he had only one more task to do. The Masters had diverted to narcotic business and it was giving them a lot of money, very soon they would rise again, and that was the last thing Mafians want. They want the complete downfall of the Masters, complete eradication... and he knew exactly what he would do... and when he would do it. The Masters would be expecting another stock of dope from Bangkok, it would be the largest stock they had ever imported....

He picked his unlisted phone and dialled the central police station. He knew the officer in charge of the Masters' case.

'May I speak with Inspector Paul,' he spoke in a very unperturbed manner. He was in no hurry, this was the last straw.

'Who is on the line, please?'

'Just tell him, I have an information about the Masters.'

As soon as Alan Giwa found a phone booth in the airport, he called his house in Nigeria. Joseph, the man in charge of Jennifer answered the phone and Alan ordered him to release Jennifer.

When Alan Giwa reached Pretoria, he checked into a comfortable hotel, not five-star but something close to it. He would cut down expenses because he wanted to settle in South Africa. It would take time to find a job, but somehow he had to get a residence permit.

Joe's address was not a prestigious one but it didn't take Alan time to find it, just three days.

On his fifth day in Pretoria, Alan decided to call at Joe Mbakwe's residence. Precisely 7.00 p.m., Alan pressed the doorbell.

When Marina Mbakwe opened the door she was so shocked, and lost for words.

'Who is it dear?' Joe said getting up from the couch. He came to the door. He was shocked to see Alan Giwa on his front door but miraculously for him, he kept a straight face.

'What do you want?' Joe said.

'Are you inviting me in? I want to talk with you,' Alan said.

'I have no business with you.'

'I know,' Alan said coming inside the sitting room without an invitation. Joe didn't comment. He closed the door.

Alan continued, 'Chief Okoh sent me here to kill you. I didn't want to, all I wanted to was to escape from Nigeria and I used this opportunity to come to South Africa. Nigeria is a very dangerous ground for any Master. Ever since the boss died and the bombing of the company there has been great instability among the Masters. They have diverted to narcotics and it is bringing in a lot of money. Next week they are expecting a stock of cocaine from Bangkok, the largest they have ever imported.'

'Why are you telling me all this?' Joe asked.

'I don't know.' Alan paused hesitantly, 'Joe, I admire your courage, you really tried in eradicating the Masters. Since the past four weeks, I've been trying to put the finishing touches to your work, the drug venture was really booming for the Masters and very soon they would rise in full force, but that was the last thing I wanted, so I started giving off information to the Mafians. They too would do anything to see the total downfall of the Masters as well as the Vikings. I just hope they would finish up the job of eradicating the Masters.'

There was a very long and uncomfortable silence.

'I don't trust that man,' Marina said when Alan left their house, 'I strongly impeach his motives, I think he is trying to put us into a dangerous safety, to make us feel very safe, then when we relax, he will strike. I think we should call Inspector Oladipo and inform him.'

'Inspector Oladipo is in Nigeria, we are in South Africa and he can't do a damn thing about the situation, besides, Marina, strangely, I believe Alan. I don't know why, but I believed him.'

Joe Mbakwe was right in believing Alan. A month later, Inspector Oladipo called with the greatest news of all.

'Guess what?' Oladipo's voice boomed into Joe's ears 'we've finally nailed them. Paul received an anonymous phone call that gave us all the information we needed to nail them. We sent one of our smart policewomen and she acted as a decoy to trap them. It is really a long story but the long and short of it is that the Masters have gone down the drain. We have arrested Chief Okoh and six others apart from Larry. Others are still at large. The Nigeria Drug Law Enforcement Agency has burnt the tons of cocaine they stored in their warehouse. The pharmaceutical company that supplies them with amphetamine has been closed down, the owner disappeared.'

'You guys really did a lot of work. I'm glad it is over for you guys.'

'What do you mean 'for you guys'? You are not sounding as happy as I do,' Oladipo remarked.

'It is not over for me, don't you understand? It has left me with scars, I don't think I'll ever feel safe in my life again, or trust anybody.... The Masters and Vikings would always haunt me in my dreams. I can still see SK Obi's face as he threatened 'The Masters will get you even if the

Vikings don't,' I can still remember clearly all the crimes....'

'It's OK' Oladipo broke him off, 'It is just a question of time, Joe... just time.'